Ans	_____	M.L.	_____
ASH	_____	MLW	_____
Bev	_____	Mt.Pl	_____
C.C.	_____	NLM	_____
C.P.	_____	Ott	_____
Dick	_____	PC	9/05 _____
DRZ	_____	PH	_____
ECH	7/08 (childs)	P.P.	_____
ECS	_____	Pion.P.	_____
Gar	4/05	Q.A.	_____
GRM	_____	Riv	10/08 _____
GSP	8/06	RPP	_____
G.V.	_____	Ross	2/09 _____
Har	1/07 (Berg)	S.C.	3/05 Robinsson
JPCP	_____	St.A.	_____
KEN	_____	St.J	_____
K.L.	02/08	St.Joa	_____
K.M.	_____	St.M.	_____
L.H.	_____	Sgt	_____
LO	_____	T.H.	_____
Lyn	_____	TLLO	_____
L.V.	_____	T.M.	_____
McC	_____	T.T.	_____
McG	_____	Ven	_____
McQ	_____	Vets	_____
JUB 5/07	_____	VP	_____
_____		Wed	_____
_____		W.L.	_____

Easeful Death

Easeful Death

Eileen Dewhurst

Severn House Large Print
London & New York

This first large print edition published in Great Britain 2003 by
SEVERN HOUSE LARGE PRINT BOOKS LTD of
9-15 High Street, Sutton, Surrey, SM1 1DF.
First world regular print edition published 2003 by
Severn House Publishers, London and New York.
This first large print edition published in the USA 2004 by
SEVERN HOUSE PUBLISHERS INC., of
595 Madison Avenue, New York, NY 10022

British Library Cataloguing in Publication Data

Dewhurst, Eileen
  Easeful death. - Large print ed.
  1. Cults - Fiction
  2. Moon, Phyllida (Fictitious character) - Fiction
  3. Women private investigators - Great Britain - Fiction
  4. Detective and mystery stories
  5. Large type books
  I. Title
  823.9'14 [F]

  ISBN 0-7278-7313-X

Printed and bound in Great Britain by
MPG Books Ltd, Bodmin, Cornwall.

One

Mary Mason wouldn't have seen her daughter if an obstruction on the line hadn't brought her train to a final stop at Billing-on-Sea. She was on her way home to Sea-minster after an enjoyable afternoon in the central London shops, and the carrier bags on her lap and around her feet that bore witness to its success had her swearing under her breath as she gathered them together and staggered laden on to a wind-and-rain-battered alien platform already lit against the dreary winter dusk.

'Sorry, sir! Very sorry, madam!' The ticket collector, warm and dry behind his window, was at least trying to look concerned for the small straggle of disconsolate ejectees poking their tickets and passes at him. Weighed down by her bags, Mary was un-able to break into enough of a sprint to secure one of the three taxis at the rank just outside the station, and was forced to stand for a long fifteen minutes exposed to the equally matched elements with no more defence than the unbecoming plastic bonnet she made herself keep in jacket pockets against such a predicament. There was also the necessity of keeping the tops of her bags closed against the weather, and by the time a taxi arrived she was in something of a temper, although still just able to reflect ruefully that the majority of the world's population was considerably worse off at that moment than she was.

'A-a-a-h!' Disposing her bags on and around her once again, then snuggling back into her seat for the fifteen-minute journey, Mary Mason's normal equilibrium was immediately restored.

Only to be lost far more dismayingly a few seconds later.

As the taxi turned from the side road into which she had emerged, and entered the slow convoy passing the main entrance to the station, Mary had time to observe a small group of young people arrayed outside it and attempting to hand leaflets to those going in and coming out. Each wore an unwavering smile, however aggressive the brush-off, and this had just put Mary in mind of the ever-polite representatives of various minority religions who called on her at home when, with a jolt of shock, she realized that one of the girls was her daughter Samantha.

Mary paused abruptly with the taxi window a couple of inches down, her first

instinct to call out to Sam quickly smother-
ed by a second, that it would be wiser not to
make herself known.

As the taxi gathered speed, so did her rush
of reactions, but she was halfway home
before she realized, to her surprise and with
a sense of sadness, which reaction was
paramount: her unfamiliarity with the smile
Sam had just been directing at a succession
of strangers. How long was it since that
smile had been directed at *her* – or at anyone
else, in Mary's sight, until now? So long,
Mary realized then, that she couldn't
remember the last time her daughter had
returned her smile, or when she had given
up hope of its eliciting at least a reciprocal
stretch of the lips. At home these days,
Samantha didn't even go through the
motions: she tore into the kitchen on school
mornings with the look of sulky concentration that was still on her face when she
mooched up to the fridge on her return; and
at weekends it was the same, except that her
entry into the kitchen was a mooch at both
ends of the day, and started an hour or so
later. Between times, Samantha was either
out, ostensibly with friends, or shut up in
her room to the accompaniment of a sound
track that at least – the one bright spot
Mary could discern among her increasingly
uncomfortable thoughts of her daughter –
wasn't as loud or as aggressive as she knew

7

from contacts with other mothers and sit-coms on TV it might well have been.

What had happened to the bear hug and the smacking kiss on ear or hair that had once followed Sam's bouncing entry into the kitchen – to those evenings when they'd sat together on the sitting-room sofa, enjoying or scoffing at television and exchanging uninhibited comments on the respective highs and lows of the day behind them, more like sisters than mother and daughter?

Now, Mary was suddenly forced to admit, they were more like strangers.

She found herself as shocked by her own behaviour as by Sam's. Why had she just accepted what her daughter had become, accepted the constant low-level pain of Sam's apparent indifference to her, the sense of hopelessness that things would ever revert to the sunny days that now evoked in her, ridiculously, a sense of nostalgia, of lost paradise? She should have resisted the change months ago, when it had started, but she must have been grieving so self-absorbedly over Barry's death that she'd been unaware of its beginnings. Now she thought about it, with this new and unpleasant sense of shame, it could be that the force field protecting her grief had excluded even her daughter. Not only had the girl suddenly to live without a father; maybe her mother, too, had withdrawn from her into her own suffering.

They'd wept more than once in each other's arms, and she'd cut down her hours with the agency, Mary protested to herself with sudden fierceness; the change in Sam couldn't have happened abruptly – she couldn't have changed one morning from the open, loving girl to the sullen miss who slouched about the house without giving or receiving. The bear hugs couldn't suddenly have become unspontaneous. It was a relief to Mary to remember that it was she who had inaugurated them for the decreasingly hopeful time until they ceased, but it was too painful to probe her memory any further. All at once, it now seemed, she had found herself living with this sullen girl who never smiled and seemed scarcely to have the energy to exchange the time of day with her.

Yet here had been Sam, only five minutes since, handing out leaflets to strangers with smiling eagerness – Sam, who had been eager for nothing for so long that, to her mother, it had become her norm.

It was still raining heavily, but Mary didn't bother to hold the tops of her bags together as she trudged between taxi and house. The smile she had seen on Sam's face at Billing station, she thought wearily as she unpacked her purchases and threw them on to the bed

9

with scarcely a glance at them, would not be there when she came home.

Bracing herself for the contrast between what she had just seen and what she was expecting, Mary poured herself a gin and tonic. She usually had one at the time she started thinking about making dinner; it marked the transition of the day into the evening, a small agreeable ritual that tonight she hoped might also be a small prop – alongside a telephone call to Maurice; after she'd seen and talked to Sam and perhaps – she didn't yet know – told her that she had seen her outside Billing station...

'Hi, darling!'

A mumble from the hall. Then feet on the stairs.

'Sam!'

The feet lagging to a halt. 'What is it?'

'How about coming to say hello? At least putting your face round the door?'

No response, but the sound of the feet slowly descending.

'What is it?' Samantha repeated, obeying the letter of her mother's second suggestion; then, as Mary looked at her without a reply, coming slowly into the sitting room and pausing short of her mother's chair. 'Something wrong?'

'I don't know. I hope not. Are you all right, Sam?'

A wide-eyed, unfriendly stare. 'Sure. Why

shouldn't I be?'

'I just wondered ... You always look so un-happy, these days. When you're at home, at any rate. Would you rather be living some-where else?'

The surprise in Sam's face, and then the fleeting panic, were the first emotions Mary had seen there for a long time. The panic gave her a flicker of hope that her daughter might not be as discontented at home as she pretended, and the hope persisted as she took in the exasperated response to her sug-gestion.

'No, I wouldn't. Unless *you'd* like it.'

'Oh, darling ... Of course not; I'd hate not to have you here. It's just that lately ... you hardly ever speak to me, let alone smile at me. So it's not really surprising that I've started to wonder—'

'I'm fine, Mum, just fine. So leave it, um?' Sam was starting back towards the door, scarcely bothering to turn her head. 'I'll be leaving school in the summer. If I get a university place I'll be off anyway, and if I don't ... I hardly think I'll be looking for a job in Seaminster.'

'No, of course not; I wouldn't expect ... Sam!'

'Yes?'

Mary's voice had been suddenly so emphatic that the girl turned round as she responded, and stood still.

'Sam,' Mary repeated, more softly but not about to retreat from what she had all at once realized she was unable to resist saying. 'I saw you this evening, outside Billing station. There was something on the line, so my train couldn't go on to Seaminster and I had to get a taxi.' Mary was studying her daughter's face as keenly as she could without letting it show, and saw alarm leap into the beautiful eyes (as a baby they had appeared so large in her little face, everyone had remarked on them), to be followed by a brief and inward-looking smile that could only indicate that her mother had reminded her of why she had been standing outside Billing station. But the alarm was instantly back, together with a new defensiveness.

'All right, so you saw me.'

'Handing out leaflets. Smiling and going on smiling even at the people who brushed you off. What's it about, Sam? As I've seen you, and know there's something, you might as well tell me what it is.'

An elaborate shrug, which Mary suspected wasn't a reflex. 'OK.'

'So do me the courtesy of sitting down while you talk to me. Is it a religion?' Mary asked, as Sam slowly complied, the sullen look back in her face.

'Religion?'

Mary had thought many times in the past

months how wonderful it would be to hear her daughter laugh again, but this bitter, condescending yelp gave her more pain than pleasure.

'Yes. Religion,' she responded sharply. 'Is that what it is? I hardly think leaflets advocating double glazing would have fixed that big smile on your face.'

Oh, why had she resorted to sarcasm, the refuge of the insecure?

'Church on Sundays? Our Father who art in heaven?' At least Sam was showing the same weakness. *'That* mumbo-jumbo!'

'You'd hardly be handing out leaflets on behalf of the Church of England, Sam; you must know that wasn't what I meant.'

'What did you mean, then?'

'I meant ... I meant some sort of organization to do with life and death and ... and other really important things. And please don't repeat my words in that scornful tone of voice. I'd rather you showed me one of the leaflets.'

'Is that an order?'

'Of course not. Oh, Sam, why do you always look for the worst in what I say and do? I'd just like to know what ... what it's all about.' She'd been going to say *what you've been drawn into,* but stopped herself in time. 'Something that had you smiling in the face of brush-offs must be pretty important to you.'

'It is, Mummy!' For an aching moment Mary saw the flush of enthusiasm in her daughter's face, the sudden light in her eyes and upward curve of her lips; but they were dull again as they came to rest on Mary's. 'OK,' Samantha said listlessly, 'I'll get you one. But you won't like it.'

'You don't know that.'

'Oh, but I do.'

'So try me, then.'

At least, Mary comforted herself as Sam dragged out of the room, the child hadn't looked scared, or even really reluctant – which had to mean that whatever she had got caught up in wasn't something likely to evoke a parental ban.

On its surface appearance...

There was still, thank heaven, Maurice.

Chief Superintendent Maurice Kendrick was at home with his wife and daughter when his sister rang. His working day had seen the satisfactory winding-up of a particularly difficult case, and he was feeling uncharacteristically mellow and contented, turning a glass of good brandy in the fingers of his left hand and, when Jennifer went complainingly upstairs to finish her home-work, stroking Miriam's breast and shoulder with his right.

'I wonder how much longer she'll be content keeping family mealtimes, appearing actually to enjoy her parents' company?' Miriam mused aloud. 'I mean, Samantha was like her once, but now ... Neither you nor I have ever said anything, but sometimes she's been so sulky and ungracious poor Mary's apologized for her. I wonder if she's like that outside the family?'

'Probably not. But having said that, young peer groups tend to look miserable these days. I was talking to one officially a few days ago, and remember thinking as I looked at them that they were victims of a collective lack of a sense of humour.'

'Except for the blessed few who do something worthwhile together, like playing in a youth orchestra or making furniture. Thank heaven for Jenny's violin! At least Sam draws rather well.'

'Yes. We'll have to hope that brings her out of it eventually. Along with getting older and surely a bit wiser. And she *was* very close to her father. I've wondered sometimes lately if she's taking it out on Mary because she's still there and Barry isn't.'

'Mary tells me she wants to read Fine Arts—'

'That could be – hell!' Kendrick cast a malevolent look at the suddenly vocal instrument on the table beside the sofa. 'Can't I have *one* evening?'

'It could just be for me.'

But after saying 'Oh, hello,' Maurice kept

the receiver at his ear and looked steadily more grim and concerned as he listened to what Miriam could just hear was a female voice.

When they'd got back together, she had had to get used all over again to her husband's habit of very rarely using his interlocutor's name; but his half of this particular conversation was so monosyllabic, so strange, that her frustration eventually brought her to her feet, walking about the room, twitching flowers and slightly moving ornaments.

Finally, in what was his only complete utterance, Kendrick said, 'Yes, I think I do know someone. Leave it with me, Mary, and I'll come back to you. In the meantime, try not to worry. D'you want a word with Miriam? She's here.'

At the end of what Miriam could hear was a hesitant response her husband said, 'OK. She'll understand. Goodbye,' hung up, and turned a long brooding look on his wife.

Eventually she broke it, went round behind the sofa and shook his shoulders. 'Maurice Kendrick! Mary said I would understand, so she must have said you could tell me whatever she rang up about. So please do!'

'I will. Come and sit down. Mary's afraid Samantha has got involved with some religious sect.'

'What on earth makes her think that?'

'Her – Mary's – train finished at Billing today when she was coming home from Town – something on the line – and she got a taxi and saw Sam standing outside Billing station with a group of other young people, handing out leaflets and smiling, whatever the response. I think it upset Mary all the more because – as we've just been saying – Sam isn't too generous with her smiles nowadays.'

'Sam saw her?'

'No. But Mary tackled her about it when they were both home, and Sam handed Mary one of the leaflets. Willingly enough, Mary said, but reading it didn't reassure her.'

'And she's just read it to you. What's the gist of it? Is it a police matter?'

'I don't think so,' Kendrick responded slowly, 'although I can't say I like the sound of it.'

Miriam moved a little closer. 'You wouldn't like the sound of anything with the merest whiff of religious eccentricity. All right, don't sigh at me like that. I won't say another word until you've told me what Mary told you.'

'It makes no reference to a god or gods. Apparently it offers a "sure, safe path" – Mary was quoting – to the afterlife when the time comes.'

'Don't be so uncomfortable about it. After all, you *are* only quoting ... Sorry. Carry on.'

'Thank you. The sect, group, call it what you will, offers to put punters in individual touch with someone on the other side – someone who's died – who will ensure that when they die a strong hand will be waiting to grasp theirs and pull them safely through the gap. Across the bridge is the eponymous image. Well, just The Bridge. That's what it calls itself. I thought my niece had more sense.'

'Maurice Kendrick, your niece has recently lost her father. So if someone's swearing blind that he's waiting for her ... No question, I hope, of the bridge-crossing looking so desirable it's being brought forward?'

'Not on paper. But I don't like the sound of it any more than Mary does. Nor the thought of my niece smiling and smiling without cause. It smacks of an altered state.'

'But it's still not a police matter, Maurice.'

'Not on the surface.'

'But you're obviously not prepared just to let it go on.'

'Of course not. It's got to be looked into, although at the moment it doesn't justify even a covert police presence.'

The brooding look was back and Miriam returned it, hearing a lavatory flush start up and die away upstairs before breaking either the mutual gaze or the silence. Then she

18

said, 'Phyllida Moon,' and saw Maurice's face lighten.

'It seems just the job for the Peter Piper Agency,' he said.

'Yet you were wary of suggesting it. Maurice, I know you admire Phyllida Moon, and it doesn't bother me. I even know you've come to like her. And you'd be horribly abnormal if there was no woman apart from me that you liked or admired. But that's not the only reason for your wariness, is it? It's about having been obsessed with her multiple identities long before you met her as herself. Which is why it was "Miss Bowden" that you shouted out once in your sleep, not "Phyllida".'

'Oh, darling.' Maurice laughed as he hugged her, amused now by the memory of his old hang-up and experiencing anew, as he did every few days or nights, his joy that his wife had come back to him. 'Your perception is staggering. Yes, I was obsessed. Despite Dr Piper's assurance that he had only one female field worker on his staff, I just couldn't quite believe him and carried the puzzle round with me like a crossword clue I couldn't solve. I mean, one moment a daily woman, the next an American sophisticate.' For which non-existent woman, to his chagrin, he had felt a little more than admiration, an absurdity he could scarcely confess to himself, let alone to his wife.

19

'Once I met her as herself, the obsession was over.' He hesitated. 'But she *is* a remarkable woman, all the more so for being so ... well, so neat and contained – no evidence of an ego but able to adopt a raging one at the drop of a hat.'

'She'd be best with a fairly quiet one if you put her on to this sect of Sam's. If you do, as it isn't a police matter, you'll be going to the Agency for the first time as a member of the public.'

'Yes.'

It seemed like a logical progression, Kendrick thought, as he turned on his side an hour or so later to go to sleep: first, dismay at being faced with one of Miss Moon's characters when a private investigation turned into a murder investigation, and he had discovered her in situ; then grudging and irritable admission of her usefulness, turning to acceptance of it, leading on to his actually seeking the assistance of the Agency on a recent case. As the final stage of that acceptance, he himself, as Plain Maurice Kendrick, about to seek Phyllida Moon's help on his own behalf...

His short-fused impatience was keeping him awake and, to overcome the inner restlessness that was making him want at the least to toss and turn and at the most to wake Miriam, he passed Phyllida Moon's weird set-up vis-à-vis the Peter Piper

Detective Agency before his inward eye. Sleuthing in character, she would inevitably receive requests from both men and women for her current persona to continue to be available after its work was done, or in ways outside its professional brief, and the anonymity so vital to her work – and, Kendrick suspected, to her own very private self – could never have survived without an accommodation address. Kendrick knew, from his own experience on the last case in which the agency had been involved, that Dr Piper had received an appropriate reward from the manager of the Golden Lion Hotel across Dawlish Square from the agency, for whom he had brought a potentially destructive scam to a close: John Bright had offered Phyllida Moon a permanent room in his hotel, where she could sleep over if necessary, create her cast of characters and, crucially, disappear without trace from the clutches of an enemy, intrusive friend, or would-be lover. John Bright had never, Dr Piper had told the Chief Superintendent admiringly, asked a single question about the women who came and went from Miss Moon's small office-cum-bedroom, and the staff who shared his secret were as efficient and discreet as he was himself. Always, Phyllida herself had told Kendrick the night he had had a drink in the Golden Lion with the American sophisticate, she came to the hotel as herself and departed as herself from it, so that her home remained as anonymous as she was. That anonymity was her ultimate disguise, and Kendrick thought he knew how fiercely she would guard it.

And would relish the challenge he still had to wait too many hours to offer her.

Two

Peter's call to Phyllida about Chief Superintendent Kendrick's request felt as initially intrusive as the call Kendrick had received from his sister, but it warbled into a very different kind of privacy. Phyllida was sitting in one of the small gardens, each uniquely different – and invisible – from the others but connected by a narrow gap in hedge or wall, which formed the most charming feature of Seaminster's Botanic Garden.

Well wrapped against the sunny cold of a March afternoon, she was reliving her recent past from a white iron seat set against a hawthorn hedge in the rose garden, the garden her husband had designed and over which less than a month ago she had scattered his ashes. Dr Jack Pusey had become terminally ill so soon after his elevation to the Botanic Gardens in Edinburgh, and had done so much over so long to establish and nurture Seaminster's few acres as their Director, that he had asked her to bring him finally back.

She could sit here now without weeping, although half an hour earlier she had surprised herself in tears as she looked across the Garden's café to the table where the big man with the kind eyes had been sitting over a hearty meal the first time she had spoken to him as herself and not the red-headed Scotswoman she had been when they had fallen in love ... Oh, it wouldn't do not to be working, Phyllida thought as she raised her eyes to the cloudless blue sky, not to spend so many of her waking hours as other women, with her sorrow in enforced hiding behind their temporary concerns and her need to protect them. It was a blessing that made bearable – even beloved – the hours of leisure when she licked her wounds at home or, as today, bathed them in the place that for so many years had been Jack's life.

So the voice of her mobile phone was an intrusion, although always, now, there was the possibility it might be Jack's son James at the other end of the line...

'Phyllida Moon here.' The one situation in which she could safely announce herself into the void: James and the staff of the

Agency were the only people who had her number.

'Sorry, Phyllida' – Peter's slightly breathless voice, exaggeratedly apologetic, and a vivid mental picture of his thin eager face, the fair hair falling over his forehead. 'I know you're off duty, but I couldn't resist trying at least to get hold of you to report another first.'

'And what's that?'

'An individual called Maurice Kendrick ringing for an appointment. No intermediary, and the words "Detective Chief Superintendent" not passing his lips. He wants the Agency's help over a problem to do with his niece. Specifically, he wants Phyllida Moon's help. What d'you think of that?'

'Perhaps we should think of it as a logical progression. Has he told you enough for you to decide if it sounds interesting?'

'Well, no. Not yet. I just thought it was interesting per se.'

'So it is. I'm as intrigued as you are. When's he coming in?'

'Tomorrow morning. He asked for nine thirty and I said I thought we could manage that.'

'Of course. Everything all right today?'

'In your department, fine. In mine too, I suppose, though I've been watching the Bentham building for so long frostbite is threatening. Where are *you*?'

24

'In the Gardens.' She had barely hesitated.

'I'm sorry. I didn't think...' That stab of jealousy he was ashamed of, all the more because it was jealousy of a dead man; but a dead man, Peter was gloomily certain unless he had drunk too much, who would for ever remain a husband.

'If I really hadn't wanted to be disturbed, Peter, I'd have shut off my mobile. I'm glad you told me; I'll enjoy a few hours of fantasy before we find out what it's all about. Did he sound bothered?'

'Would he? And he didn't waste any more words than usual. It's a bit of an endorsement, though, isn't it?'

'It is indeed.'

'I must let you return to your ... I must let you go.'

'All right, but I'm glad you rang. Miss Bowden will be with you soon after nine in the morning' – the severe spinster, ten years or so older than Phyllida, who enabled her to appear on view in the Agency and, increasingly, take her own cases. She appeared there as herself only in its books.

Which was more than Phyllida Moon's appearance in the recent television series *A Policeman's Lot*, she mused, her communion with Jack temporarily broken and her thoughts growing less painful as they moved away from him. There, her role as the policeman hero's private-eye sister had been acknowledged in the credits by yet another pseudonym; she had remained aloof from all the publicity surrounding a hit new series and, once her initial anxiety about being recognized had proved to be without foundation, she had been amused as well as relieved to see that John Bright and his staff, the staff of the municipal library where she did research on a long-ongoing book about women and the stage, plus, it seemed, everyone else who surrounded her life, had not seen even a likeness between her and her small-screen character; and yet, Phyllida reflected on a rare stab of self-satisfaction, in that role she had worn no prosthesis...

She was lucky, she supposed: if she hadn't had the excuse of her vital anonymity she would have hated the personal publicity, the interviewing, the signing of autographs – all the things her fellow actors had relished – perverse creature that she was. Sighing, Phyllida got to her feet, stamped them against the cold, and walked briskly towards the exit. Jack would be glad, she thought with an inward smile, that her professional self could still vie successfully with her personal self, and would carry her through an evening of the sort of speculation she had not lost the ability to find enjoyable.

Kendrick had known, of course, that he would be seeing Miss Bowden in Dr Piper's office rather than Miss Moon, but he was still visited by the sense of frustration he had been ashamed of in the past when Miss Bowden, or another character equally uncharismatic, had blocked his view – first of the sophisticated American woman and, now, of the less obviously but more satisfyingly attractive Phyllida Moon. At least he was spared Miss Bowden's flat northern vowels: Phyllida spoke in her own soft low tones.

'How can we help you, Maurice?' she enquired, as Jenny, having brought posh coffee in (a cafetière, cups and saucers instead of mugs, milk in a jug) and served it, closed Peter's door on her departure.

Kendrick spread his long legs in front of Peter's one large armchair and fixed his brooding gaze on Miss Bowden's annoying face. 'It's tricky. Not your possible role, Phyllida – that I hope is fairly clear – but the situation. My sister's daughter – only child – is seventeen and going through a sulky, uncommunicative stage, which I'm told is usual these days. I don't have personal experience of it as yet: my daughter's only twelve...' Kendrick hoped his involuntary shiver of apprehension had gone unnoticed. 'Anyway, a couple of days ago my sister was leaving Billing station in a taxi and saw Samantha handing out leaflets with a group of other youngsters, all wearing invariable

27

smiles however ungracious the response. Sam didn't seem scared or even wary when Mary faced her with it at home later and asked to see a leaflet, which we both hope is a good sign, but how can one tell without...'

'Without sampling the product,' Peter offered into Kendrick's second pause.

'Precisely. I was confident you would grasp my point pretty quickly. It's a ... well, a sect of some kind, I suppose, that calls itself The Bridge. Here's their bumph.' Kendrick pulled a leaflet from his breast pocket and tossed it down on the desk. 'You'll see ... they claim to make it possible for the living to contact an individual member of the dead as a sort of personal guide to steer them through – over, according to their chosen image, a bridge – the fact of death and deliver them safely on the other side.' Both Peter and Phyllida noted that the Chief Superintendent's normally pale face had reddened, and heard the increasing reluctance in his voice. 'All nonsense!' he went on briskly. 'But I want to be sure it isn't wicked nonsense.'

'Of course!' Peter responded enthusiastically. 'And there *is* a disturbing implication: I don't imagine they say anything in their brochure about hastening the desirable process you describe, but they wouldn't, would they?'

'No. They wouldn't.' There had been a

flash of fear across the dark, deep-set eyes.

'But that's very much a worst-case scenario,' Peter added hastily.

'I hope so. But a possible scenario it is, and one you've just made me face. Thank you, Dr Piper.'

'I hope we can do more for you than that, Chief Superintendent.' It was Peter's turn to redden, in annoyance that his reflexes had caused him to forget his determination to follow his new client's lead and not refer to Kendrick's occupation; but the client's face had relaxed into a rare smile.

'It's plain Maurice Kendrick visiting you this morning, Dr Piper; and as Miss Moon and I are now on first name terms, I suggest the same for you and me, except on paper.'

'Thank you. Maurice.' Peter wished he had more time in which to savour the highest point in the life of the Agency to date. 'You know I'm Peter.'

'Indeed. So, Peter, you'll see in the leaflet a few dates of coming meetings of The Bridge.'

'Bit of a milk-and-water title,' Peter said.

'A safe one. Use the word "death" and the connection with euthanasia is automatic. If "death" was in the title, I might even feel I could investigate myself, professionally. So they've thought it out. Their venue's the tiny one-time fleapit – called, inevitably, the De Luxe – in Barton Street.' Kendrick paused to look a question at Peter's evident surprise.

'I know it,' Peter said. 'I even went there as a child – nine old pence on a Saturday morning.' He looked a question, in his turn, at Phyllida, who, mentally out of character and unvigilant, had let her sense of surprise and satisfaction show: she had not known until that moment that Peter had set up business in his home town. 'The least salubrious end of Seaminster these days,' Peter went on ruefully, when she had smiled and shaken her head. 'But it was always a bit on the grotty side. I wonder how long this Bridge set-up's been going. Barton Street isn't much of an address.'

'It doesn't say in the leaflet, but Sam told her mother a couple of years or so.'

'Is there a god or gods involved?' Peter asked. 'I mean, does one have to qualify through a prescribed kind of worship, or good behaviour, for this helping hand from the other side? Sorry, that's why you gave us the leaflet; and the dogma, or lack of it, isn't immediately relevant to what we're able to set up for you.'

'I gather from my sister that Samantha expanded on the brochure a little, when her mother questioned her. Apparently the promoters of the cult see death as a transition to another life in the light of a law of nature.'

'So why the need of a helping hand?'

Phyllida asked.

'Ah. That I can't tell you. But I suspect it's the weak point. They could hardly go so far as to suggest that without that hand no one will make it; it would be like saying there are only a handful of people in a world of millions who can conform to the last natural law.'

'I can see the attraction,' Peter said slowly. 'Near certainty, for the true believer, that he or she won't end in oblivion, and the means to ensure that certainty. Insure it, in fact. Without, so far as we know, having to earn eternal life the way the orthodox religions require. But there has to be some catch.'

'Which is where my sister's anxiety begins.' Kendrick pulled himself upright and leaned forward. 'Now, before we go any further – start discussing how Phyllida can best present herself and so on – I have to ask you both if you have any reservations about helping me to investigate a group of probable weirdos we already know have one power: the power to fix an immovable smile on my niece's normally sulky face.'

'Phyllida?' Peter asked, trying to hide his anxiety.

'No reservations, Maurice. I only hope what I can do will be of some use.'

'Good. That's very good.' Neither Phyllida nor Peter had ever seen clear satisfaction in Maurice Kendrick's face, but both were

31

aware of some tension leaving his body as he leaned back and stretched his long legs. 'Perhaps you'll draw up your usual form of contract, Peter. Phyllida, I expect you'll need time to decide the best sort of character to adopt. If you want to discuss it with me, fine, but if not, if you feel you don't need to, I'll be happy with that, too.'

'I'd like to discuss it. Or them. It doesn't have to be just one character.'

'I hadn't thought of that. Though God knows I should have done.' Both Peter and Phyllida jumped slightly at Kendrick's sudden bark of a laugh as he recalled the 'is-she-one-or-is-she-many?' threshing of his thoughts that had even kept him awake during the earlier cases in which they had encountered one another. 'But to start with...'

'I should say someone unobtrusive, to look and listen and not be noticed by the folk at the top. Reassuring and approachable, though, so that a young woman, say, sitting next to her and wanting to talk out her excitement, would feel she could. Middle-aged to elderly, untidy, unsmart, comfortable...'

'You know her already, don't you?' Kendrick said.

'I've used her already. Which doesn't mean she'll look entirely the same next time. But yes, I know what makes her tick.'

'I'll get her a real identity,' Kendrick said. 'And somewhere to live. I don't think staying at the Golden Lion would fit, but of course it'll remain your bolt hole. Oh...' For the first time since his arrival in Peter's office, Kendrick looked undecided.

'What is it?' Phyllida asked.

'I was assuming ... I don't want to tread on Agency toes. Would – could – it be part of your service to find Phyllida's characters somewhere else to live than the Golden Lion?'

'It has been,' Peter said. 'Although it comes pretty expensive. In this case, though ... Well, I imagine you'll have the better facilities. Oh Lord, I'm sorry. I was forgetting you're not here as a policeman.'

'I am a policeman, though,' Kendrick said, looking without expression from one to the other of them. 'And I can provide accommodation as well as an identity that would bear investigation.'

'So please do both,' Peter said, after a glance at Phyllida elicited a nod.

'Very well.' Kendrick permitted himself another brief smile. 'This is a worthy cause.' One he would have no difficulty commending to his esteemed Detective Sergeant Fred Wetherhead, the one member of the local force who knew of his chief's professional liaison. 'Perhaps we can aim for the next meeting but one, which will give us just short of three weeks to be ready for it. I'll come back to you with details of identity and living accommodation as soon as I can. I can't choose, of course, but I'll hope to give Phyllida's first character as ordinary a name as possible. And rented accommodation as salubrious as can be found. And when I come back' – Kendrick fixed his reflective gaze on Phyllida – 'I shall be interested to learn about the woman who will be going to that first meeting.'

'She'll be here, Maurice, next time you visit us.'

'I know she will.' Kendrick uncoiled from the armchair, and Peter on his feet looked small to Phyllida for the first time. She herself, although a tall woman, felt the strain in her throat as she looked up at the Chief Superintendent – who wasn't, as she had expected, striding towards the door.

'Is there something else?' Peter asked.

'Well ... It's just occurred to me ... If your Steve Riley had a scout round at the meeting we shan't be ready for ... not as a member of the congregation, or whatever they call themselves, but maybe by the door when they arrive and/or depart. At Billing station...'

'It had just occurred to me, too,' Peter said. 'And Steve will love it. I'll report to you following that meeting. At your home address, of course. Maurice.'

34

'Of course.'

Now Kendrick made his way swiftly to the door. Seeing Jenny's hopeful face turned towards them as he opened it, Peter asked her to show Mr Kendrick out and closed it on her eager rising from the computer.

Phyllida had crossed to one of his two identical sash windows, and he joined her there, where for a few moments of silence they watched the line of the sea visible beyond the serration of rooftops below them. The anticyclone that would have been a summer heatwave was still above them in its cold, still, late-winter brilliance, and the sea, scarcely less blue than the cloudless sky, was flicked on the summits of its wavelets with yellow-gold from the mocking sun. Phyllida felt for the moment almost at peace, and Peter realized sadly that he was almost accustomed to the depressing contrast between her physical nearness – her sleeve had just brushed his arm – and his knowledge that, as a woman, she was the other side of the world. But both of them, as always, were warmly aware of their working camaraderie, and both, this morning, despite their respective sorrows, were unable to dodge a slight sense of buoyancy and incipient adventure generated by Kendrick's visit.

And a fear of the danger it could bring.

Three

Steve began his evening rush-hour drives past Billing station a week before the next advertised meeting of The Bridge, and had drawn only two blanks before he saw the girl in the photograph Chief Superintendent Kendrick had left with the Agency, handing out leaflets in the company of three or four other smiling young people.

Samantha Mason hadn't been smiling when the photograph was taken, but Steve was good at likenesses and instantly recognized the long bright hair, the set of the head even above a swathe of scarf, and the arresting structure of the facial bones. As good-looking, he decided instantly, as the photograph had promised, even with that determined stretch of the mouth ... Determined it had to be: Steve witnessed two brush-offs as the traffic bottleneck forced him to idle, one resulting in a leaflet falling to the ground. The smile was undimmed when Samantha straightened up after crouching to retrieve it, like the animation in the large dark eyes, so cold in the picture but so warm now in the glow of the station light above the girl's head.

It was probably the warmth in the eyes, Steve reckoned as he drove reluctantly on, that had taken the goose over his grave in the moment he recognized it: Samantha Mason's smile wasn't pasted on. She believed in what she was doing.

Peter had told him Mr Kendrick wasn't expecting him to attend the meeting, and Steve had assumed this was because the DCS was thinking of agency time and expenses rather than because he was afraid Steve's presence there might in some way jeopardize Phyllida's presence at the later meeting. When Peter had given him the assignment, he had been mildly relieved that his brief was for an outside job only, but having seen Samantha Mason, and the expression in her eyes, he found himself wanting to make more of it; and because there was just the possibility that it was not Kendrick's concern for agency time and costs that had decreed the ban, Steve decided, as he quickened his pace away from the station, that he wouldn't trouble to enquire about the Chief Superintendent's motives. He would, perhaps, simply attend the meeting...

He drove past the station each rush hour until the meeting date, and each time Samantha Mason was standing there, even on the day the anticyclone had crumbled into a bone-aching scythe of rain-sodden wind and it was hard to believe that as a result the temperature had risen above freezing. This time, the fair hair was plastered dark to Samantha's head, her hands looked swollen and her fingers fumbled as they tried to separate the damp leaflets, and Steve's streak of knight-errantry was activated, so that his still tentative idea of attending the meeting hardened into a certainty that he would.

'I've scouted round Barton Street, Guv,' he told Peter the next morning. Much impressed by the third rerun of that ancient classic *The Sweeney*, Steve had insisted on a clause in his contract with the Agency permitting him to call his boss 'Guv', even though they were not policemen and their manor was not a part of London. 'There's a chippy just about opposite with a couple of tables in the window, which'll be useful. I thought I'd hang about on the pavement while they're going in. Then be in the caff when they come out.' It was an omission, rather than a lie.

'That sounds all right. Try not to be cloak-and-daggerish when you're on the pavement, especially when you take your pictures: we don't want anyone to look at you twice – as much for your own future anonymity as in the interests of this

38

particular case.'

'Understood, Guv.' It was unlike the Governor to be reminding him these days of the basics of street behaviour, but Steve swallowed on his resentment as he realized from his own unaccustomed fear of screwing up that Peter's overanxiety had to come from the extraordinary fact that their client was Seaminster's most senior policeman. The admonishment evoked a few qualms over his decision to exceed his brief, but he managed to suppress them – he'd cultivated his unmemorability for just such a venture, and his governor knew as well as he did that he'd been sent into arenas far more dangerous to that unmemorability than a seat at the back of the old De Luxe behind a load of fanatics hypnotized by what was happening up front.

When Phyllida that morning looked in on her friend Sally in the lending section of Seaminster's municipal library she was not, as she usually was, on her way up to the reference section to pursue her intermittent research for her much neglected book on women and the stage. With Peter's blessing, she had come specifically to see the only person in Seaminster apart from the staff of the Golden Lion and Detective Chief Superintendent Kendrick who she knew was aware of her double life. It had not been intended that Sally Hargreaves should join the small circle, but in one of her more hazardous cases Phyllida had had to turn in an instant from a frail old lady to her own undisguised self in order to save Sally's life, and they had been friends ever since.

Phyllida found Sally at her usual station behind the central reception desk, a bright cynosure for borrowers' eyes with her lively, very pretty, and frequently smiling face. There was no one at the desk as Phyllida went up to it, and Sally was looking thoughtful as she consulted the computer screen beside her; but when she sensed a presence and turned to the counter, she was instantly alight with pleasure.

'Phyllida! How lovely! And how conscientious. About to work through your lunch hour!'

'Yes, but not upstairs. I've come to take you out to lunch.'

'And that's work? Oh, dear.'

'I hope you won't be saying that when you've heard what I'm going to ask you.'

'Intriguing. So please don't keep me in suspense. Come on, what is it? Oh...' Phyllida's grave look and a finger briefly at her lips made Sally break off, looking a mixture of excitement and disbelief. 'It's to do with ... that?'

'Yes. Let's go to Vernon's. With luck we can tuck ourselves into a corner before the crowds break in. You're still on early lunch?'

'Yes!' Sally glanced at the big clock above the door, then hopefully at the door itself. 'Monica should be here any minute to take over.'

'Right. I'll browse until she arrives.'

Phyllida barely had time to renew her regret at not having enough time to read for pleasure before Sally was gripping her elbow as she shrugged into a raincoat. 'Come on, then!'

There is a lane leading directly from Seaminster's Victorian municipal complex to the High Street, but the day was so wild that the women were cold, wet and wind-blown when they gained the fuggy warmth of the restaurant. It was barely past noon, but the bright, pastry-filled window had already attracted a considerable clientele, most of it as close to the passing scene and the counter as it could get, so that Phyllida and Sally were able, as Phyllida had hoped, to find a vacant table in comparative isolation at the back.

Sally, despite her slenderness, had a fine appetite for food, and usually immersed herself in the menu the moment she sat down; but today she hadn't so much as glanced at it when she demanded to be told what it was all about. 'You never admit to anything even when I'm pretty confident I've found you out, like when you were getting over your gall-bladder op in that dodgy nursing home last summer. Before you went – I'm sorry. Oh, Phyllida, I'm sorry.'

'Don't be. It's all right. Before I went to Edinburgh and married Jack. That's what counts, Sally. I'll never not want to talk about it. About him. But now ... about why I've asked you to lunch.'

Sally had picked up the menu in her embarrassment, but cast it down unread. 'Give!'

'The Agency's just taken on a worried widowed mother who's afraid her teenage daughter is becoming too involved with a cult. She stands outside Billing station in all weathers handing out leaflets and never stopping smiling. At home she's surly and doesn't smile at all, which makes it all the more disturbing. I'm going to a meeting of the cult in a couple of weeks, and as it's been decided that I'll be an elderly lady, Peter and I thought it could be useful if I took my attractive young niece, who might even get to speak to our client's daughter. Are you interested, Sally?'

'Do I like shrimps Marie Rose? Oh, Phyllida, that's fantastic!'

'I'll give you the same protection I give myself. You'll emerge in disguise from the Golden Lion – just a wig,' Phyllida added, in response to Sally's ecstatic wriggle, 'which in public you'll take off only when you've come back to the hotel. You'll be living with your aunt – I don't yet know where – for the time being, having quarrelled with your flat mate and not yet found another place.' Phyllida smiled into the animated face. 'Better make it a female flat mate, so that you can announce to all the panting young males that you have a serious boyfriend. Sally, I do hope Jeremy will feel able to go along with all of this. I'll promise him personally, if you like, that the only time you'll be out of my sight in public is if you go to the loo. And no doubt I'll accompany you there too.'

'You've got it all worked out!' Sally whispered, goggle-eyed.

'It's second nature by now. But wearing a wig and having a different surname doesn't mean not being careful.'

'Don't worry, I will be – while doing my best, of course, to make contact with your *subject*.' Sally's voice underlined the PI jargon word as she grinned at Phyllida. 'What's this cult about? Devil worship? Black magic?'

'Nothing sinister on the surface; but the fact that it's brought that persistent smile to a sulky face ... Samantha Mason's mother is worried, Sally.' Mary Mason, née Kendrick; but there was no way that crucial fact could come out. 'Here's a leaflet. Tuck it away and read it in private. Now, let's order before the place gets impossibly busy. And when you've told me how Jeremy is.'

'Jeremy's fine!' The sudden radiance again, as always when the subject of conversation was Sally's partner.

'Any ... developments in the offing?'

'You're starting to sound middle-aged, Phyllida; you'd better watch it. Marriage, you mean? Babies?'

'I suppose I did mean something of the kind.'

'OK. We *have* started to think about a baby. And I suspect we'd both prefer to be married by the time one arrives.'

'There you are, then. Oh, Sally, I'd be so pleased for you.'

'Thank you. Phyllida...' Sally was embarrassed again, now closely studying the menu.

'Yes?'

'I've wondered ... if you and Jack had considered ... You're still young enough...'

'Thank you. We considered to the extent of letting nature take her course. She must have decided it wasn't a good idea.'

'Oh, Phyllida. I'm so sorry. And for being such a clumsy fool.' Phyllida had banished it swiftly enough, but Sally had seen the instant of pain in her face.

'It's all right. I've been waiting for someone to ask me that, and I'd rather it was you,

Sally, than anyone else. And Jack's son James is turning out to be a model stepson. I'll tell you about him when we've ordered. We'll talk about the other thing in your house or mine, except I'll say now that if Jeremy objects, you mustn't go against him.'

'Jeremy object? That's *funny!*'

'I wasn't making a joke, Sally.'

'No, I know. But he won't object. Honestly.'

'Good. I'll have a baked potato with prawns Marie Rose.'

'Me too. I don't know why I ever bother looking at the menu.'

The weather was no better by the evening and, sitting at a table in the window of the Barton Street chippy, Steve suspected the scrum in the shabby narrow doorway of the De Luxe to be due as much to the cold wet wind as to faith or curiosity. He also suspected that, had he been at Billing station on foot any evening during the past week and Samantha Mason's smile had for a brief moment been for him alone, he would have found himself in Barton Street now whatever the contents of the brochure over which their hands would have made brief contact...

He got to his feet as the scrum diminished to a dribble, paid for his coffee, and sauntered across the narrow street in the face of his instinct to dash for shelter from the wind-driven rain.

Beyond the De Luxe door was an immediate strong smell of damp clothing and two smiling young people, a boy he thought he remembered from outside Billing station, and a girl whose face had already entered his dreams.

Following the couple of heartbeats in which Samantha Mason's real-life smile was his, Steve rode his white charger into a back seat, which he discovered as he sat down was a 'double', no doubt installed in those unimaginable days long gone when the moral climate – he had read somewhere with amazement – had made it so difficult to get body against body with one's beloved, in public or private...

Steve experienced a brief pang of conscience as he remembered his faithful girlfriend Melanie, but as always managed quickly to dismiss it. He was there for her, wasn't he, every Saturday and Wednesday night (except when work, or something he told her was work, intervened)? And as yet he'd never given her the affirmative answer she was constantly seeking that he was faithful to her.

Already there was no more than a sprinkling of empty seats and, as he had hoped, Steve found himself feeling comfortably anonymous even though the house lights were on. They were dim and dirty, but he was able to see the people still filing into the seats in front of him, and that the majority of them had come alone. On an inward snigger he was reminded of a documentary he had once seen about the old Windmill Theatre in London, whose proud boast had been that, even during the bombing in the last war, it had never closed, and which had nurtured so many of the great comedians in the intervals of what would now be considered risibly timid girlie shows. The raincoats and trilby hats had given way to jeans and jackets – worn by more women than men – but with many of the arrivals there was the same watchful furtiveness as they warily sat down, no doubt hoping that a friend or neighbour would not have succumbed to the same instinct of curiosity or hope. There were also one or two nervously twittering groups of girls – there, Steve decided, for a dare. There were older people too, but Steve found himself disturbed by the preponderance of the young. All right, he shared their likely lack of interest in orthodox religion, but he didn't share the current widespread and sometimes frenzied search for a spiritual dimension to replace it.

The girl and the boy who had been at the door were keeping pace with each other along the aisles to each side of him, the girl

47

so near his end seat he felt the cool swish of air as she passed him and imagined he could smell scent. They were climbing the matching steps on to the platform with military precision and starting in precise unison to clap their hands as the curtains, golden light illuminating their lower folds, slowly parted.

'A small fat guy came on first,' Steve reported to Peter and Phyllida in Peter's office the next morning, when he had confessed to having exceeded his brief and been shriven for it. 'Gave out notices and so on and had an ordinary chair to sit on when he'd finished. The top chap had a sort of miniature throne, a bit like that Masonic chair they've got on show in the library lobby. Not that he needed it. You could see in a minute that he was the Jesus chap.'

'I'd prefer not to have that particular description in your written report,' Peter said, with the brief touch of severity it was still necessary to mete out to his junior field worker now and again. 'But tell us why you used it.'

'Charisma. It came off of him in sparks. Arms thrown out, head thrown back, face on fire. The other chap ... well, I suppose the contrast made Mr Jesus – sorry, Guv, the Big Chief – look even wilder. *He* didn't smile; he just sat turning his head from his chief to the audience, all stern and watchful. He introduced himself as the business manager, and he wasn't pretending to be anything else.'

'So what *happened?*' Peter asked.

'Well, the Chief opened the proceedings with a sort of run-through of what he believed in. There was some clapping when he'd stopped speaking, but I got the feeling some of us were too self-conscious to let ourselves go. Then there was a sort of a prayer session where everyone bowed their heads because he did, having been told to try to find themselves a friend on the other side, apparently with his assistance. I heard a few grunts and groans around the place but nothing too near to me, thank the Lord, and when that was over his number two asked for questions.' Steve paused, suddenly looking embarrassed. 'For goodness sake don't ask me what it was all about, Guv; let Phyllida sort that one out. It was something to do with making sure you got to the other side when you died, but I was concentrating on the personnel rather than the text.'

'Fair enough,' Peter conceded. 'But you chose to go in, so you can run us through the order of play.'

'Righty-ho. I got the feeling some of the questioners might have been planted, and the questions chosen in advance, and it was the business chap who decided which ones should be taken, and when to stop. That took us through almost an hour. There was an old joanna on the platform, and an old woman came up and played some sort of song – the words are on this bit of paper, which the girl and boy came down and handed round.' Steve laid a crumpled single sheet on Peter's desk. 'Nothing about any sort of a god, but it sounded like a hymn. Then the Chief wished a revelation on everyone and retired whence he had come. After that his business manager gave the notices out again – I've written 'em down – and another two youngsters were appointed for duty at the next meeting.'

'You kept an eye on Samantha Mason, of course.'

'When I could. It was too gloomy to see anyone or anything properly, more so 'cos of the dazzle on the stage, and she was sitting somewhere round the front row, so I only saw her when she was on her feet.' The wistfulness in Steve's face and voice had Peter and Phyllida exchanging quizzical glances. 'Anyway, you wanted a low profile.'

'I did indeed. So what was your overall feeling about The Bridge, Steve?'

'Kind of spooky,' Steve offered, after a moment's thought. 'I mean ... everyone acting as if it's normal to have a dead mate; no revivalist stuff – shouting, arm-waving and so on – except from the Chief. That business manager, looking as if he should be at a board meeting but going along with it

50

all ... Yeah. Spooky.'

'I'm getting curiouser and curiouser,' Phyllida said. 'You said the Chief, Steve. Is that what the others called him?'

'No, that's me, when the Governor said I mustn't ... *They* called him the' – Steve glanced down for the first time at his dog-eared notebook – 'the Enabler.'

'Phyllida?' She had shivered, and Peter had noticed.

'I'm all right. It was just ... That's a far more powerful and sinister title than Chief, or even Messiah. What does he enable?'

'Safe passage across the divide,' Peter said – 'to quote from his brochure. Which fails to give him a proper moniker, or an address. Anything more, Steve?'

'Nope. I slipped out – not the only one – as the final applause got under way, just ahead of the money men moving into position against the door; and I was back in the window of the caff by the time the big exit began. I ordered egg and chips, and it and the Enabler and his business man appeared at about the same time.'

'Money men?'

'A couple of big fellows carrying bowls to collect voluntary contributions from a grateful congregation.'

'Um. Miss Mason and her fellow duty officer came out with the chiefs?'

'No. The oldsters just let the door close

51

behind them and headed off out of sight together. That's when I got my pictures. The young ones came out ten minutes or so later.' Both Peter and Phyllida interpreted the brief cloud across Steve's face as a distaste for the thought that they might have stayed behind for longer than was strictly necessary. 'And locked up before going off the other way.'

'Together?'

'I couldn't see more than a few yards, but it looked like it. I'd've followed the big chiefs if I hadn't thought I ought to wait and see the place closed up. And make sure Samantha Mason came out in one piece. She *was* my subject, Guv.'

'I'm glad you remembered it, with all the excitement. You can follow the leaders after the next meeting, when Phyllida's on the inside job. Find out if they stay together, and if not, where the chief makes for. All right?'

'Great, Guv!' Steve's sombre face had lightened as Peter spoke, but now took on a look of fond reminiscence. 'Those chips in the Barton Street caff! They were some of the best I've ever tasted.'

Four

It was pure coincidence that brought Mary Mason out of her living room into the hall at the moment her daughter and a young man came into the house through the front door, but Sam offered her mother a glare of sullen suspicion. The young man, whom Mary hadn't seen before, gave her a look of friendly speculation – and a brief frisson, because he made her think of her lost Barry the way he had struck her the first time she had seen him: slight but tall figure, bespectacled, earnest face, good intentions shining from large, anxious eyes. A boffin, she had thought at once, and so he had been, but such a clever one. His shyness and preference for the hidden role had gained him universal respect...

It was more than time for her to stop going off into reveries about Barry when people were waiting for her to speak.

'Well, hello,' she heard herself saying, trying to sound matter-of-fact rather than sprightly, and immediately afraid she hadn't managed it – one of the main miseries of her current relationship with Sam was finding herself so regularly on the defensive.

'Hello!' the young man responded, on a flash of smile. However eager he was to please, the one thing Mary was certain he wouldn't say was that her daughter had told him a lot about her. Perhaps Sam had, but it wouldn't be the kind of thing he would want to pass on. 'I'm Denis Young. You must be Sam's mum, she looks so like you.'

'Thank you. I'm flattered.' *There I go again*, Mary thought ruefully. *It ought to be Sam saying that.* But Sam wasn't saying anything, just shifting from foot to foot and glancing with exasperation towards the stairs. 'Well, I mustn't keep you. Are you going to listen to music?'

'I don't think so,' the boy said, looking at Sam. 'So we won't be disturbing you.' His voice was a disappointment with its flat London whine, dispelling his evocation of the young Barry.

'I wasn't worrying about being disturbed,' Mary said. 'I was just being interested.' *Just being pathetic, for God's sake.* 'Do you share Sam's new interest?' she plunged on, not knowing what she was going to say until she'd said it. 'The Bridge, isn't it? She's shown me—'

'For heaven's *sake*, Mum!'

But the boy's smile had returned, and remained now radiantly in place. 'Yes,' he

54

said reverently, 'The Bridge. Perhaps we can persuade you to come to a meeting. It'll transform—'

'We haven't got much time,' Sam interrupted brusquely, 'and I don't think my mother would really be interested. Sorry, Mum, but we've a lot to get through, organizing the next meeting, and then we're out for the evening.'

'Of course. Off you go. Can I make you a sandwich to keep you going?' she heard herself asking as they started towards the stairs. 'And/or some coffee?'

'Well, that's awfully kind...' Denis glanced at Sam, who shook her head impatiently. 'It's OK, though, really.'

'Right. So you'll be late home, Sam?' Mary hadn't meant to say that, either.

'I don't know. I shouldn't think so. But don't wait up.'

'Don't worry, dear. I'll go to bed when I'm ready.'

The only bit of spirit she'd shown, Mary acknowledged with annoyance as she watched the two pairs of legs disappear round the curve of the stairs. Surely growing up didn't have to be a growing away, she protested to herself on a strengthening shaft of anger as she went back into the living room, unable to remember why she had gone out of it. A constant, hovering hostility. Was it this Bridge that was causing it? Or had the malaise that had gripped her daughter for the past difficult months made her vulnerable to the siren voice of the cult? Which was the cause and which the effect?

The welcome anger died, was painfully replaced by loving pity, as Mary recalled The Bridge brochure. *Someone on the other side ... A strong hand to grasp ...* Sam's father's hand ... The child was reaching out, swallowing guff in her eagerness not to lose contact with the father she'd so dearly loved.

Why did she have to withdraw her love from one parent while she lavished it on the other? Mary's anger returned to sustain her through the hour her daughter and the young man remained shut in Sam's room, and even allowed her a grim inward smile at the sudden realization that her concern over her daughter entertaining a man in her room had no sexual dimension: her beloved Samantha was suffering from a hunger of the soul, which Mary suspected could be currently excluding other appetites.

What she, Mary, was suffering from was exclusion from her daughter's hopes and fears, the reinforcement of herself by Samantha, every time they met, as an irritating irrelevance – the cruel negation of a mother's role...

The wording of her thoughts rekindled her anger, and when Samantha put her head round the living-room door on her return just after eleven, she found her mother still in her chair and meeting her gaze with a look of cold authority (Mary had had to work on it) that had Sam sighing but at least pausing.

'Come and sit down,' Mary said.

'I'm tired, Mum.'

'So am I. We'll both go to bed in a minute. But sit down first.'

Repeating and exaggerating the sigh, Samantha cast herself down on the sofa. 'So what do you want to talk about?'

'You. I'd like to know why you've withdrawn your friendship from me.'

Sam's eyes widened, and Mary believed she could have scored a small hit.

'Come on. Tell me.'

'There's nothing to tell. I haven't *withdrawn* anything.'

Another mocking repetition of her choice of word, perhaps the most hated ploy of the new Samantha; but this time her mother hoped it might be defence rather than attack.

'So why do you assume I couldn't be interested in your Bridge? Are there no older people involved?'

Uncertainty, now. Something relatively precious, in this icy climate. 'Yes, there are. Our ... our leader's older. And the ... his second-in-command. And some of the

57

members. But you're so ... I mean, you think you know where you are, who you are; you wouldn't be interested in radical ideas. Even when you were young you'd never have gone on a demo.'

'Maybe not. But that doesn't mean I have a closed mind, Sam. Especially where you're concerned. Tell me about your young friend Denis.'

'For God's sake, Mum! He isn't my *young friend*.' There it went again, and Mary could feel her anger stealing back. 'He's a person. A fellow member of The Bridge. So don't worry, I'm not about to jump into bed with a boy with an accent who didn't go to public school and who lives in a high-rise council flat.'

Sam's last words had Mary checking her anger with a mental squealing of brakes, just as it was about to surge forward. 'There's nothing wrong with living in a high-rise council flat,' she managed to respond, evenly. 'Whereabouts is it?'

'Need you ask? On the wrong side of Billing, of course. The notorious Pickford Heights. But don't worry when we hold a business meeting there: it's recently had a facelift and some of the more subversive elements have been forcibly relocated.'

'I thought he seemed like a very nice boy. What does he do?'

'He's a clerk or something in the local job

centre. Anything else you'd like to know? I don't think he's in a position to support me.'

'All right, Sam. Does your Bridge have any political affiliation?'

'God, Mum. The Bridge is to do with life and death. Didn't you pick up *that* much from the brochure?'

'Yes. But one priority doesn't always exclude another.'

'Well, The Bridge does. No one's concerned about politics. Or class. They're irrelevant.'

'Like religion?'

'Yes. Like religion, too. Religion's as manmade as everything else. Life after death is a law of nature that The Bridge makes people aware of. It's a different kind of life, the life that's lived on the other side of death, and The Bridge doesn't pretend to know what it's like. It just knows it's there, and that we're bound to reach it if we have help from the other side.' *My father*.

Sam wasn't suggestible, Mary tried to comfort herself, so there could be no other reason for her to have got caught up in this nonsense. Dangerous nonsense?

'How does The Bridge know this?'

'*Mum!* The Enabler – our leader – had a personal revelation. It was so real and so strong it left him able to pass it to other people. It's wonderful; it means you'll never be lonely, even in solitary confinement. It makes you independent. Whatever people do to you in this world, they can't touch you in the next.'

'But if you don't make contact with the next world now, it means you never get there?'

'Oh, Mum!' – but a little less vehemence. This could be the sticky bit. 'You should get there, you're meant to get there, but it isn't an easy crossing and some people ... well, they sort of fall through the gap.'

'Off the bridge.'

'That's right!' Sam had answered eagerly, and took a few seconds to revert to a suspicion that her mother was taking the mickey. 'That's exactly right,' she repeated aggressively. 'And when you arrive, you've got a friend.'

'How much d'you get to know about your friend while you're still here? Do you acquire just one?'

'Just one, yes.' For a heart-rending second, Mary saw her daughter's wistfulness in her eyes, but she had no hope of Sam coming clean that she was picturing her father; and, in fact, she was going swiftly on: 'You don't know anything about him – or her – except for knowing they're there.'

'And you've found yours, Sam?'

'Not yet ... It isn't easy; you have to be ... well, sort of open ... For God's sake, Mum, not *sexually!*' Mary, to her intense annoyance, had let a flicker of alarm cross her eyes.

'No, darling, I realize that. It's just ... all rather difficult to understand.'

'Of course it is, if you haven't listened to the Enabler. He's wonderful! He makes it all so clear.'

The way Hitler did; but Winston Churchill did, too, Mary consoled herself, as she saw that Sam was getting restive. She got to her feet.

'Thank you for telling me so much, dear. I can see how important it is to you, and I do hope it goes on bringing you comfort.'

'Yes, it does bring comfort.' Braced for a sarcastic repetition of her unwisely chosen word, Mary was taken aback, then flooded with a foolish sense of hope. Perhaps this strange obsession that had taken hold of Samantha could serve to bring them back together...

She started towards the door. It would be good to sleep on that sense of hope, rather than dash it by trying to build on it now and failing. 'Goodnight then, darling. Sleep well.'

'Goodnight, Mum.' For the first time in weeks Sam kissed the proffered cheek before slouching out of the room. Mary went slowly back to her chair glowingly aware of the brief point of contact, and listened for the usual loud closure of her daughter's bedroom door before picking up the telephone.

Maurice answered.

'I know it's late,' she said, 'but I may have something for you. Sam brought a young man back with her today who seems very much involved in her Bridge thing, and who lives in Pickford Heights. I don't know how you're managing your investigation, but I thought the information might be useful.'

'More useful than you can know, Mary.' Maurice never sounded excited, but she thought there was a throb in his voice. 'Thank you. Anything else?'

'She just kissed me goodnight – well, brushed the cheek I offered with her lips. And she talked a bit about the theology of her cult. Not uninteresting. I suspect it all stands or falls on the personality of the man at the top.'

'That sounds familiar; but at least this demagogue doesn't seem to have an evil agenda – on the surface. I should know more soon, Mary.'

'I've every confidence.'

When Kendrick was shown into Dr Piper's office on his next visit to the Agency, Miss Bowden's place was occupied by a shapeless lady of indeterminate age with untidy grey hair, thick spectacles on a nice plain face, and a kindly smile. Kendrick had considered himself ready for anything, but to his chagrin reacted with an annoyance that evaporated only when the kindly smile grew mischievous.

'We caught you!' Peter exclaimed gleefully. 'You can't deny it; it was in your face. What's this old biddy doing here, when we've business to discuss?'

'I don't deny it.' The smile was now so beguiling Kendrick's chagrin was fast disappearing. 'I have to welcome it. If *I* was taken in, all geared to being deceived ... I'm very satisfied.'

'I'm glad to hear that, Mr Kendrick. So I hope you'll soon give me a name.'

'I'll give you one now. You're Miss Emily Lubbock' – whose voice was as soft as Miss Moon's but more breathy, and with a touch of Scots – 'and you're about to move into a flat on the fourth floor of Block B of Pickford Heights.' Kendrick threw an envelope down on the desk. It was bulky, and landed with a clunk. 'That contains the keys, papers validating Miss Lubbock's entitlement to them, and one or two other things that will be helpful. There's nothing about Miss Lubbock's first incarnation, and don't ask me.'

'Of course not,' Peter responded quickly.

'My sister found out by pure chance that a young man her daughter knows from The Bridge lives in the Heights. It was tremendous luck: to find out where a Bridge supporter lives, and that it's the sort of place where it was comparatively easy for me to get hold of a flat.'

'There *is* luck in the private-eye business,' Peter responded enthusiastically to the long figure sprawled – he thought more negligently than hitherto – in his largest office armchair. 'It doesn't operate in every case, of course, and I don't think I've ever had it twice during one, but it's always on the cards. This is the first time, though, that it's come from the client.'

'This client has to have more pull than most, although the plea of police business isn't an open sesame; but it does cut down on the whys and wherefores of an inquiry.' Kendrick thought fondly of his DS Wetherhead, of whose willingness to take on a few extra-curricular duties – and even safely devolve some of them – he had no doubts. 'I've managed to get you on to the floor where this young man – one Denis Young – lives. You're between him and the lift and stairs, so you can be at your front door, polishing the knocker or something, when he comes past, no doubt armed with leaflets.' Kendrick reddened. 'But that's up to you, Phyllida,' he said, almost apologetically. 'How you go about making his acquaintance is your part of the business.'

'With a little bit more help from you, if

you can give it. Do you know what he does? If he goes to a regular job?'

'He works in the local job centre – clerking – which should have you engaged in conversation within days at most. We've fitted the largest peephole we could find in the front door.' Conscientious as he was, and always had been, on behalf of his force, Kendrick found himself wondering uncomfortably if he was paying seriously undue care and attention to this first investigation on behalf of himself. 'Phyllida, Peter...' He pulled himself slightly upright. 'You haven't shown your reactions to Pickford Heights, but they can't have been favourable. I can tell you, though, that the blocks have been recently upgraded and the worst elements moved elsewhere. It won't last, I'm afraid, but at least at the moment the lifts work; and they've eliminated a lot of those notorious walkways. Anyway, I'm not, of course, envisaging Phyllida living there full-time. Or even part-time. I suggest you invent a relative you stay with a lot, if anyone comments on your absence.'

'I will. I've already invented a niece – in real life a young friend who lives with her partner in Seaminster. She should be of help with the younger set.'

'And she's privy to your double life?'

'Only because I once had to change in a hurry from age to comparative youth to ...

well, to...'

'To save her life,' Peter supplied.

'When we'd both got over the shock, we found we wanted to be friends. I don't have a great many locally, Maurice, as you can imagine; but I make up for that in the quality of those I do have.'

The warmth of the accompanying smile had Kendrick saying 'Thank you' before starting to wonder if in fact it was including him. 'I'm sorry,' he went on quickly, 'I can't assume—'

'You can.' Phyllida was surprised as well as pleased by both oblique declarations, and put her own uncharacteristic forwardness down to the easy persona she was inhabiting: Miss Emily Lubbock was quite without unnecessary inhibitions. 'Sally's to be staying with her aunt for the duration, and she'll go with her to The Bridge meeting. I'm giving her the protection I give myself, of course: she'll emerge disguised from the Golden Lion and shed her disguise there, and she'll be as much a resident of the flat at Pickford Heights as I am. She's pretty and outgoing, Maurice, and she'll take any opportunity she can get to speak to your niece. So we have a couple of chances of contact.'

'And an expansion of Steve's outline report,' Peter said. 'He's good on the objective stuff, but not over-empathetic. Phyllida will measure the Enabler's impact on his audience – without, I hope, succumbing to it herself.'

'I'm not personally all that suggestible,' Phyllida assured them. 'And I think Sally's pretty secure psychologically too. But I'll keep a good eye on her.'

'So your idea is to accept a leaflet when you encounter Young on the landing, and take your niece along with you for the ride. Because...?'

'Because ... Oh, well, because Denis Young *is* young, and so is Sally. And because the aunt just likes the niece's company, and her comments on the modern world. Miss Lubbock's no fool, but she's a bit woolly in her thought processes and won't have worked it out. In fact ... *I'm* working it out as I go, and on second thoughts she'll show the leaflet to her niece, and it'll be Sally who says come on, auntie, for a lark.'

'I like it,' Kendrick said. Phyllida's and Peter's heads tipped back as he uncoiled. 'But both of you be careful.'

'I'm looking forward to it,' Phyllida said, when Kendrick had gone and she and Peter were standing together at the window nearer to his desk. Before Jack, she had never accompanied him on his contemplative prowls to the view of the sea, or taken one of her own; but having once been forced by the threat of tears to turn away

from him, and choosing the sea, she sometimes, now, got up when he did and stood
beside him to share his contemplation,
usually in silence.

And without the slightest idea, Peter each
time reflected mournfully, of the effect on
him of her close presence.

As Miss Emily Lubbock, though, she
made the intermittent contact of their
elbows a lot less provocative and his
thoughts were almost free of her as his eyes,
as always, drew in the solace of the horizon.

'Kendrick's right, though. You must be
careful, and instruct your friend Sally
likewise. I can imagine that sort of people
are so keen to gain recruits, if they get their
eye on you, they won't easily let you go.'

'Which is what we're aiming for. Come
on, Peter!' She had turned to him in surprise. 'I've run worse risks and come out
smiling. If they do turn out to be dangerous,
it's straight to Kendrick and the police take
over. And if they don't take notice of us,
we're wasting our time.'

'Of course. I was being unprofessional,
thinking of young Sally.' Thinking of
beloved Phyllida. But his slip had shown,
and he had to take it as a warning; and
remind himself that they were – and ever
would be – colleagues first, friends second,
and lovers nowhere.

'I'll take care of Sally,' Phyllida rallied

him, 'and she'll give the impression of taking care of me. She's totally agog. We might even have another young field worker in the making.'

A blonde Sally Lubbock accompanied her aunt that evening when she moved into Pickford Heights. Despite their facelift, the two blocks, opposing one another across a few yards of sparse and featureless grass on which a couple of plastic bags and some plastic bottles were stirring in the stiff March breeze, were deeply depressing: greyly angular, with ugly gashes of a harsh, aggressive blue proclaiming the lines of balconies. Phyllida had hoped to find an answerphone system at the outer door, but it swung open at Sally's touch and there was nothing in the lobby apart from the lift doors – more harsh blue – to relieve the squarely defining concrete.

There was also a pervading sense of damp, with undertones Phyllida didn't want to analyse, and she and Sally turned to one another on an instant, wrinkling their noses and smiling rueful smiles, as they advanced reluctantly towards the blue door.

At least the lift worked without protest and was fairly clean. Their smiles turned brave in the few seconds it stopped moving and failed to release them, and it was with an ironic sense of relief that they stepped out on to a concrete corridor, lit at each end by the remains of daylight through a small grimy window.

Blue doors again – 'A few moments ago blue was my favourite colour,' Sally whispered – and number 157 a few steps to the left, opening readily enough to the keys Maurice Kendrick had thrown down on Peter's desk.

Phyllida, from pure curiosity, had been looking forward to discovering how much, if anything, had been done by their client's unnamed minions to turn what must have been a basic set-up into something acceptable to Miss Lubbock's comparative gentility, and was touched as well as amused to find a vase of daffodils and tulips on the rickety-legged hall table. It was a pointer to the rest of the place: the furniture was indeed basic, but there were decent throws hiding the worn tweed of sofa and armchairs and the limp bedcover, and when Sally tested the beds in the two bedrooms and pronounced them nice and firm, they discovered new mattresses on the old bases, and fresh bedclothes. Kitchen and bathroom were clean, and the utensils usable without qualm. Phyllida even wondered for a moment if Kendrick had visited the place himself, before remembering a recent televised police press conference on the local news, and realizing that he couldn't have risked it.

'We'll be all right,' Sally said confidently. 'Jeremy was quite happy when I promised to keep ringing him. I wish I was staying with you tonight. Are you sure I shouldn't be?'

'No need until I've made contact with Denis Young. And if I manage it in the morning, he won't know that the niece I may mention isn't asleep somewhere behind the figure filling the doorway. Now, I'll make us some tea.' She would never say that again without remembering the nurse saying it the moment she had pronounced that Jack was dead. 'And then you must go home to Jeremy. Via the Golden Lion, of course. Reception will be expecting you, and will let you have a key to my room. Just drop the wig in the box at the bottom of the wardrobe.'

Five

The third set of footsteps on concrete since six thirty a.m. ceased short of Miss Lubbock's front door just as Phyllida was about to open it. Despite the new mattress she had slept poorly, a thread of anxiety she was unable to escape running through her fitful sleep and troubled dreams. She had set an alarm for seven, but when she accepted, just after six, that sleep was not going to return even superficially, as through the night, she decided to get up and sit close to the outer door, listening.

Since half past six she had opened it on to two approaching people: one a hurrying young woman, who offered a quick nervous half-smile as she sped on to the lift, the second a heavy-footed, thickset man whose glance had made her glad to be in so uncharismatic a disguise.

Now, at a quarter to eight, Phyllida hesitated in the sudden silence, deploring her indecision and more pleased than alarmed when her doorbell rang. Whatever the outcome, she had been shown what to do.

Miss Lubbock opened the door without undoing the chain, and peered warily through the gap. 'Yes?' she asked. 'Who is it and what do you want?'

She could see enough to answer the first question herself – Steve's photograph had, as usual, been a good one – and feel confident of the answer to the second, particularly as the young man outside was dangling a sheaf of leaflets from his hand.

'I ... Miss Lubbock, isn't it?'

'It is. But how do *you* know that, young man?'

The pale, earnest face reddened, but the

answer came promptly enough: 'I've a friend in the housing department, so I find out who's coming in so that I can welcome them.'

'Very commendable. But are they always glad to see you?'

A shift from foot to foot. 'No. I'm afraid not. Some of them, that is. Lately it's been a bit ... easier. I'm very glad to welcome you, Miss Lubbock.'

'Thank you. You're a nice, polite young man; you must come in and a have a coffee with me some time. You're off to your job just now, no doubt. Commendably early.'

'We have flexible hours. If I go in early, I can leave early.' No personal PR, Phyllida decided, no attempt to present himself as super-conscientious – which was refreshingly unfashionable.

'I see. Well, young man, you know my name, so I have no hesitation in asking you for yours.'

'Gosh, of course, I should've ... I'm Denis Young. I've been living here for almost a year, now.'

'And intend to stay?'

'Until I can afford to put something down on a flat of my own, or a terraced house. I don't want to go because of...' The red again, and a renewal of the foot shifting. 'The people here are all right. Really.' *As long as you keep your head down.* Phyllida

73

found herself surprised to see that Denis Young still had a straight nose. 'And there's no need of a steel door any more. It's just ... Well, I'd like to own my own home, and this building, the corridors and the setting ... they're pretty depressing, aren't they? I don't suppose you'll ... D'you think you'll be here for long?'

'I don't think so, Denis.' Phyllida had been thinking about her answer to that sooner-or-later question during the predominantly sleepless parts of the night. 'I've just left too big a house near London and I'm only in Seaminster because of having a young niece here while I think where I really want to go next. Having seen Seaminster, though, I'm quite attracted to the idea of staying here in a little house or, like you, a flat of my own.'

'That's nice to hear.' The flush now was of pride, as if Denis Young had a proprietorial concern for his seaside town. And perhaps, it occurred to Phyllida, one might come to feel that way if one worked for the local authority.

'Goodness me!' Miss Lubbock exclaimed. 'I shouldn't be keeping you when you're on your way to work. I'm so sorry. We'll talk another time, perhaps.'

'Oh, yes!' A wide, but slightly uncertain, smile. 'And in the meantime...' One leaflet from the waggling pack was suddenly in the other hand, and being poked at her through

74

the narrow gap. 'I'm a member of a very wonderful group called The Bridge. It's all about ... well, about life and death. And how death shouldn't be feared. We have a very wonderful leader; this will tell you about him and about our next meeting.'

'Really?' Miss Lubbock looked sceptical, although she had accepted the leaflet.

'Oh, yes. I do hope you'll come. And then you'll understand what I'm saying. The meeting's only round the corner in Barton Street. Not very salubrious, I know, but we've done up the old De Luxe cinema and it's OK, really. If you think you'd feel a bit strange, though, some of us are meeting at my flat on Friday night to contemplate together, and to ... well, to talk. You'd be very welcome to join us, Miss Lubbock.'

'As the oldest attender?'

'Well ... At my place, yes, I suppose so. But the Enabler – our leader – and our manager and some of our members ... they're quite old. And lots of the audience at the De Luxe are, too. And of course, if you think about it...' The flat voice tailed off.

'If you think that we're rather nearer to death than you young ones, then of course you're likely to have older people in your audience.' Miss Lubbock's smile now was a little mischievous, and brought the semblance of one back to the self-discomfited youth. 'When I've read your little leaflet,' she went on, 'and if I feel that I'd like to know more about your Bridge, then thank you, I'll come to your flat meeting. The only thing is that my niece is due to come and stay with me today. Would it be in order for me to bring her with me?' Phyllida had learned during her second career that a chance – unless seriously dangerous – was always worth taking. 'She's young. And curious about life, if not so far about death.'

'Gosh! That would be wonderful! The more young people we can recruit ... I mean, the more young people who see the light...' Phyllida's own shying away from the word 'recruit' had been hidden, but the boy clearly regretted using it, and she had her first pang of personal fear that the surface of The Bridge might not be the heart of it. 'Will you really come, then? And bring your niece? Eight o'clock in Flat 141?'

'As I said, young man, I'll come if I like what I read, and if I do, then thank you, I'll bring my niece – if she's agreeable, of course.'

'Of course. That's wonderful, Miss Lubbock!' Phyllida wondered idly if Denis Young ever employed any other adjective to describe what delighted him. 'So I'll hope very much to see you tomorrow night. And your niece too. What's her name?'

'Sally.' Phyllida gave him the two syllables with disguised reluctance, even though Sally had assured her over and over that the deeper her commitment the happier she would be. 'Now, off you go, young man!'

As if a nearby fire had been switched off, the triumphal excitement fell away from Phyllida as she walked the short length of the narrow hall and entered the sitting room. 'Jack,' she whispered aloud as she crossed to the wide, bleak window and stood staring across the mercifully small cluster of sixties atrocities to the varied and more gracefully roofed lower structures of central Seaminster. 'Don't let me love you the wrong way, lose my relish for my work because I miss you so much.' The long horizon, she realized as she gazed, was the sea – no more than a narrow grey line above the jagged edges of the farthest buildings, but the same sea she drew strength from when she woke in the mornings at home, and when she leaned on the railings of The Parade. It was the harsh anonymity of Pickford Heights, Phyllida decided with relief as she turned away, not Jack, that had dimmed her usually intense pleasure when she achieved more than she had cautiously anticipated.

As she looked round the room, basically furnished and upholstered long ago in shades of dingy brown, positive feeling returned to her in the shape of pity for the people who had no expectation of ever having any other roof above their heads than a square of raw concrete which within weeks of its construction had dripped dark stains on to its upper walls. As if someone had moved around the top edge, peeing down it as they went.

Amused by the graphic inelegance of her explanation of stained sixties concrete, Phyllida went restored into the little kitchen and made herself a mug of coffee, taking it through to the sitting room and ringing Peter while she drank it and kept a regular eye on that reassuring line of sea.

'It was more-than-I-deserved time,' she commented, when she had told him about Denis Young's unsolicited visit. 'That bit of luck you were telling Maurice Kendrick about. Sally'll be over the moon when I tell her over lunch.'

'No sinister subtext to date?'

'No-o-o. The lad did let drop the word "recruit" at one point, then hastily withdrew it. It was the withdrawal, I think, that gave me a second's pause, I suppose because it made me think he and his fellow acolytes could have been advised to adopt a velvet glove, which you only need if you're covering a hook rather than a helping hand. Sorry, Peter; that sounds like the most pedantic kind of deconstruction, but at the moment...'

'Don't make one of your strengths sound

like a weakness. And do be careful, of your-self and our young temp. Will I see Miss Bowden this afternoon?'

'She's lunching with Sally, and she'll be in about two. She has a less than reassuring report for her beauty-parlour client, and I thought she should present it in person.'

'Good. And I won't push any more cases your way just at the moment. Agreed?'

'Until I get some idea of how long I shall have to keep Miss Lubbock, and maybe other women, going for our distinguished client, yes, I agree. And now I'm shaking the dust of this depressing place off my feet. There isn't all that much of it, actually, and there were fresh flowers in the hall.'

'A nice gesture.' *And a pathetic reaction,* Peter told himself angrily – to feel a pang of jealousy over a bunch of flowers. Maurice Kendrick was happily married, for God's sake – it had even said so in the local press as part of a recent series of profiles of local dignitaries – and he had the dubious com-fort of knowing that the only man he would ever have cause to be jealous of was dead. 'See you later, then.'

Sally bounced up to Miss Bowden, sitting in solitary state in the deserted depths of Vernon's café, soon after twelve noon, and received a primly stern warning against too much outward sign of her delight at what

79

Phyllida had to tell her.

'Don't worry,' Sally reassured her in a stage whisper. 'And just think: we'll be going to the Barton Street meeting knowing half the people who run it! You've done wonders, Phyllida!'

'Most of it was handed to me on a plate'; and – a key constituent of the case that she could not point out to Sally – this particular client was doing as much of the work on it as were the private detectives he had commissioned. 'But you may not be free to stay the night at the Heights on Friday, of course. In which case I'll just say you have a date.'

'Phyllida! I mean Miss Bowden! You have to be joking.'

'No. You're doing this out of the kindness of your heart, and we don't want to upset your private life.'

'I can promise you you won't. We won't be in any danger, and Jeremy's that nice kind of guy who wants me to be happy even where he isn't involved.'

'That *is* a nice kind of guy. But we don't know there isn't danger, Sally. We'll have to be on our guard the whole time, however lovey-dovey the young Bridgites may appear.'

'Not let ourselves be hypnotized and come to in Timbuktu in the hands of the white slavers? No, seriously, I promise you I'll be careful, while doing my best to get on as friendly terms as I can manage. All right?'

'Of course. Prawns Marie Rose?'

'I suppose so. Not that I'm in the least bit hungry.'

'Charles Henderson,' Kendrick said to Peter, on his private line. 'Joint owner with a sister of an eighteenth-century pile that could just be called a minor stately home, seeing that the grounds, the chapel, and a couple of rooms are open to the public every Wednesday afternoon from March to October. Built by an ancestor, so this particular set of Hendersons are the real thing, too. I've gathered the brother nominally runs the place, but that it's his sister who looks after the day-to-day nitty-gritty, and acts as guide. In other words, Fifield Place is her life and her occupation, and her brother just happens to have inherited. Only half, though. The parents must have been enlightened for their time: they've handed it on as a joint tenancy – which means that, if one of the siblings dies, in that instant it belongs to the other.'

'I'm impressed,' Peter said truthfully, into the sudden silence.

'I have my sources, not all of them in uniform or official plain clothes. What's your immediate reaction to this information, Peter?'

'To send the sort of woman one never really notices to view the place this very Wednesday. Phyllida'll be glad: I feel she's rather kicking her heels waiting for the Barton Street meeting – though she's made contact with Young at the Heights, to the extent that Miss Lubbock and her niece have been invited to an informal Bridge meeting in his flat on Friday night.'

'I'm impressed, too. I'll look forward to her report. The info about Fifield Place, how to find it and so forth – that'll be with you by the morning.'

'So there's something for you to do before Friday,' Peter concluded to Phyllida, when Miss Bowden had bidden good day to a stricken client after handing over a report confirming his wife's infidelity, the impact of which it was not in her nature to try to soften; 'as one of your indistinguishable market research types, no doubt.'

'No doubt.'

For a heady moment, the adrenaline flowed at almost its old speed and volume; after Pickford Heights Phyllida had found her austere office bedroom across Dawlish Square a welcoming haven. But she must sleep for the time being at the Heights, though it was, of course, from the Golden Lion that the neat woman with the French pleat set out and drove the ten miles north to Fifield Place in the car hired by Peter from his tame garage proprietor, which to date had survived a couple of nights unmolested on the windblown tarmac beside the Heights.

The name of this anonymous woman was unlikely to be required by anyone she would encounter at Fifield Place, but all Phyllida's characters, however minor, were given names, this one receiving hers as her creator sat regarding her expressionless face in her Golden Lion looking glass, and it was Miss Muriel Chadwick who drove through the wrought-iron gates and the small, pretty park – there were deer browsing the grass among the mature trees to each side of the sandy track – turning at the bidding of an arrow within sight of the small-scale classical facade, its stone facing a warm gold in the cold, brilliant sunshine.

The car park was a rhododendron-dominated clearing hidden from both house and drive, and Miss Chadwick's car was the eighth to occupy it. Phyllida approached the house expecting to be herded into a conducted group, but when she had climbed one of the pair of symmetrical sets of stone steps leading to the front door and entered a large hall, she saw, as her eyes accustomed themselves to the comparative gloom, a lone woman seated behind a small, elegant desk near the door who was beckoning her over with a welcoming smile.

'Good afternoon! Welcome to Fifield Place!' A small, fair, fluffy woman with a delicate-featured face that was looking genuinely pleased that another visitor had sought the house out. 'The drawing room and the dining room are open to visitors,' the woman said, as she took Phyllida's proffered note. 'To each side of the hall, you'll see the notices. The chapel's open too, but to see that you have to go out again, I'm afraid, and round to the left side of the house as you face the north front. It *is* accessible from the house, of course – can you imagine all our devout ancestors trudging round the house every time they wanted to say their prayers – but, well, to get to it from the inside you have to go through some private rooms and my sister-in-law thought it was more appropriate to direct our visitors to the outside door.'

'Your sister-in-law ... You're family, then? Showing your own home? Oh!' – a drawing-back that Phyllida made literal as well as verbal. 'Forgive me,' she said, after her couple of steps' retreat. 'That's none of my business. But I saw the piece about your home and your family in the *Seaminster Gazette* a few months ago and I've been intending to visit ever since. The house is even more beautiful than the photo that caught my eye.'

'I'm so glad you think so.' The satisfaction

in the pretty face reminded Phyllida of Denis Young's reaction when she had praised Seaminster. 'And you'll know, then, that the present Hendersons are Charles and Hermione – brother and sister. I'm Mrs Charles. Yes, it is a family affair.'

She just might have been imagining it, but Phyllida thought a flash of unease had for a moment crossed the smiling face. 'How very nice!' Miss Chadwick responded. 'I think I'll have a look at the two secular rooms first.' It was time to move on, before Mrs Henderson, in the light of the boredom that must accompany such scarcity of visitors, took it into her head to make reciprocal enquiries about a visitor who had revealed herself to be a little less than idle.

'Yes. Of course.' Perhaps, now, a flash of disappointment. 'I hope you'll enjoy them.'

Nodding and smiling, Phyllida moved to the door immediately beyond Mrs Henderson's desk. It was panelled and important-looking, and beyond it was a formal and exquisitely beautiful Adam-style interior, the painted decoration on the ceiling and upper walls chiming with the painted decoration on the delicate furniture, everything comparatively small by stately-home standards and, Phyllida thought, all the more charming for that. There were fresh flowers in two appropriate places, and everything looked polished and cared for.

One member of the Henderson family, at least, was a fit custodian of this delicate survival, and Phyllida found it easy to see Mrs Henderson in the role.

Easier than the woman she encountered in the family chapel. After surveying the charms of the dining room – stronger in colour and more robust in its furnishings than the drawing room – she had passed Mrs Henderson's desk with a smile and a 'Now the chapel!' without pausing, descended the entrance flight, rounded the side of the building in the direction of a discreet arrow, pushed open a heavy door under a classical entablature set between two small stained-glass windows, and been immediately accosted by a deep female voice.

'Ah! Poor timing, I'm afraid. I'm about to close while I attend to some business.'

'Oh! Oh, I *am* disappointed. I haven't time to wait and I was so looking forward ... After readng the piece in the *Gazette*, the chapel was my high spot ... Never mind, though; perhaps I'll manage to come again.'

'Um. Look here, I can give you ten minutes. Can't have you going off looking like you've lost the Crown Jewels!'

The laugh was a bark, and the impact on Phyllida of Charles Henderson's sister was so dramatically different from the impact of his wife that she found herself inwardly smiling. This woman was tall and well made, with strength of both mind and body declaiming themselves, even in the soft and fitful lighting of the chapel interior, from a determinedly serious face.

'That's very kind of you; I really appreciate it. Did you write the article in the *Gazette*?'

An audible sniff. 'I talked to whoever did write it. Full of errors, as these pieces always are. If you ever find yourself in a position to check what's written in the papers, there's always *something* wrong. I'm getting a leaflet printed, but it's not available yet. Anyway, I can tell you what'll be in it. The chapel's the same age as the house, designed as an integral part of it. You'll notice the rather fine ceiling...'

It would all have been interesting, if Phyllida had really come to Fifield Place because of an article in the *Seaminster Gazette*, but in her current role it was just one comment from Hermione Henderson that she committed to memory.

'My brother wants to turn the chapel over to the ridiculous sect he's founded. Such sacrilege! It would involve deconsecration, and *that* would take place over *my dead body!*'

In the event, it was twenty minutes later that Phyllida parted from Hermione Henderson outside the chapel door, and began her unattended tour of the outside of Fifield Place. Access to the south face had been barred by a gated wall just beyond the entrance to the chapel, but on the other side there was an unimpeded path cutting through the grassy slope that descended from the house wall. It brought her to a couple of terraces leading down to more parkland that merged gently into a continuing landscape of fields and small farm buildings. So far, Fifield Place had been lucky to retain its setting undesecrated.

Phyllida proceeded warily towards the top terrace, and was not surprised to find herself barred from entering it by a loop of chain and a notice saying 'PRIVATE'. There was the same prohibition on access to the lower terrace, but nothing, it appeared, to prevent her from walking in the parkland below – there were a couple of small groups of people strolling about to encourage her – and look up towards the terraces.

To see, on the upper one, a lone male figure sitting motionless on one of the regularly spaced wrought-iron seats and gazing out across the prospect in front of him. The tiny but powerful binoculars she always carried in company with her tiny gun confirmed that the eyes were wide and that the expression of the face was what she could only describe to herself as a look of innocent wonderment – a far cry from the mood of the man in Steve's photograph who had electrified a hall full of people, but an alter ego which, as Phyllida studied it, appeared to her to be no less eccentric.

Six

'I don't know how you can keep so calm!' Sally protested, turning reluctantly from the panorama of Phyllida's Pickford Heights view, where she had been watching its overall grey being slowly pierced by the scattered light points of a spring dusk.

'Miss Lubbock's a calm woman. *I'm* no more calm, Sally, than I was in the days when I waited in the wings to go on to a theatre stage; but at least my nerves are wrapped up inside Emily's relaxation, which is a bit like wearing a stout overcoat you can tremble inside without it showing. When your stage is real life, and bad acting could bring about something more serious than a bad notice in next day's paper ... well, that's when you really learn self-discipline.'

'If you can. You always cry yourself down. I know *I* couldn't manage it.'

'You'll have to manage to tone your

excitement down before we leave this flat.' Phyllida studied the flushed, excited face. 'You have to be acting tonight too, you know, Sally. Remember you're a cool young woman who's teasing her old aunt into going to this meeting, while feeling no more than the merest touch of curiosity about what they'll find in Flat 141. As the evening goes on, you start pretending a bit of interest, but you go into it for a lark.'

'Yes!' For the moment Sally's face was more hectic than ever, but Phyllida was almost confident this was due to the revelation that she, too, would be playing more than a passive part in the evening's encounters. 'I just never thought of it like that. Don't worry, I can see now just how I have to be.'

'I know you can. And at least you don't look like you – not just being blonde: you've been clever with your make-up. Now, look at me: is Miss Emily Lubbock likely to ring any alarm bells?'

'Never in a million years,' Sally said decisively, studying the gently collapsed figure into which the tall, slim Phyllida Moon had mysteriously metamorphosed; 'and I can't see her getting at all openly excited about this Bridge thing. But when her niece shows a smidgen of enthusiasm, Miss Lubbock can at least be sort of humorously indulgent about it.'

'I like that'; but as she studied Sally's excited face Phyllida found her approval suddenly tinged with fear. 'Oh, Sally, I hope I'm not drawing you into something dangerous. This is the first time I've ever involved anyone outside the Agency in my capers. You can back out this very moment if you want to.'

'No way.'

'I didn't think so. But you must disappear with Miss Lubbock if I tell you to: every time she and her niece go into the Golden Lion they have the option of never emerging from it again.'

'I know, I know. Stop worrying about me!' Sally whirled across the room to the mirror over the mock fire surround. 'This wig makes me feel absolutely someone else; it's really exciting. I've always wondered what it would feel like to be blonde, and it *does* make you feel different.'

'And look it. Now, we haven't settled on what you do for a living. What about research assistant to some obscure academic? If anyone tries to probe beyond that, you can say he's a recluse and has made you promise not to tell anyone about him or his work.'

'That's great! What an accomplished fraudster you are, Phyllida!' Sally was back at the window. 'D'you know, it took a bit of nerve to say that even as a joke to the vener-

91

able Miss Lubbock.'

'Good.' Surveying the girl, who was like a light bulb in the darkening room, Phyllida reflected on that clause in Murphy's Law which decrees that the uncharismatic be attracted to the charismatic as the moth to the flame. A Denis Young type, if not Denis Young, would surely want to see Miss Lubbock's niece again. 'Sally, I think you've got to make it known at the merest suspicion of male – or female! – interest that you're happy with your boyfriend. No close-ups. So that if we decide to back off tonight – or after Barton Street – no Bridgeite will recognize you as you in the street or the library.' Phyllida glanced at her watch. 'It's time to go. Ten minutes beyond the time we were invited for. The rest of the company should be assembled. All right?' Sally had shivered.

'Yes! You just made it sound for a moment like we were about to face an inquisition.'

'So we are, Sally; but these inquisitors want to acquire us, not to find us guilty. Come on.'

They had no more than seconds in which to hear faint laughter before another dilapidated blue door was swung open and Denis Young appeared, his eyes lighting up twice, Phyllida observed: once at the sight of Miss Lubbock, and again as they took in the girl beside her. They blinked rapidly a few times before they returned to the older woman, and their owner told her how pleased he was to see them both.

'Come in! Come in! And meet my fellow members of The Bridge!'

Phyllida had had no conscious preconception of what Denis Young's associates would be like, but reproved herself mentally for her surprise at how ordinary, even conventional, they collectively appeared: it had hardly been on the cards that the eight young people relaxed on chairs, beanbags and the floor round the twin to Miss Lubbock's sitting room would have a couple of heads apiece. Forcing herself not to let her gaze pause on a happy-faced Samantha Mason, Miss Lubbock passed them all in brief smiling review while Denis presented them with the two strangers. A question within seconds from one of the girls told Phyllida that membership of The Bridge was not obsessional enough to exclude a normal curiosity about the world they were making sure they would safely quit.

'Where's your place, then, Sally?' The questioner was a strikingly attractive girl with long, straight black hair and pale, perfect features, whose relaxed length along another brown carpet suggested that she was tall.

It was Sally's blooding, and Phyllida had to summon all Miss Lubbock's calm philosophical disposition to still the beating of her heart.

Sally grimaced. 'Right now it's here with Auntie. I had a fall-out with my flat mate a few days ago and moved out.'

Phyllida's trained antennae thought they detected a slight general stir: of course, if a Bridgeite could persuade a potential recruit to accept a share in his or her home, there would be a much stronger possibility of securing her – something she hadn't thought of, and for a moment she had to fight against an unfamiliar and potentially debilitating sense of professional self-doubt.

She was over-reacting, however. Sally didn't have to – wouldn't – accept any such offer.

'Too bad,' said another girl sympathetically. Her hair was short and mouse-coloured, and she was sitting neatly on a small chair.

'They say that loss of one's home is up there with bereavement and divorce as the biggest causes of stress,' Denis Young pronounced earnestly, his speculative gaze on Sally. 'But let me introduce us to you, now. I'll just give first names at this stage; they'll be enough to remember. This is Marian' – indicating the mousy girl – 'this is Roma' – the girl on the floor – 'and this is Stan.' Stan, Phyllida thought, had the look of an *idiot savant* with his wide expressionless gaze,

94

flickering fingers, and restless body squirming about the armchair into which he seemed to have been flung – the one person in the room, she decided, who fitted the stereotype of a member of an esoteric sect, and she found herself recalling the wide-eyed figure of his leader gazing out across his family acres, whose stillness had seemed as eccentric as this young man's constant movement.

'This is Colin, Roma's ... er ... friend.' Any man selected by the exotic Roma had to be of some interest, Phyllida reflected; and Colin looked quite interesting in his own right, strong-faced and wearing a quizzical smile. 'This is Sam, our newest and youngest member...' The bespectacled gaze appeared to switch with some difficulty from Sally, but as it fell on Samantha Mason it softened afresh, confirming Phyllida's impression of Denis Young as highly susceptible to the general phenomenon of young female charm. 'And this is Charlie.' With her hacked-off hair, combat gear and uncompromising expression, Charlie looked as butch as her name, save for the heavy breasts across which she had folded her arms as if in an attempt to deny them.

'Let me see. Who haven't I ... Ah, Felicity! And Tom!' The girl and boy sitting slightly back from the group, their position in the room, it occurred to Phyllida, reflecting their comparative lack of interest in anything in it beyond themselves – they had to disengage their mutual gaze in order to smile and nod towards the newcomers.

'They've just got engaged,' Roma drawled. 'Hence the mutual admiration. They'll get over it, won't they, Colin?' The comment sounded less barbed than the words, and was accompanied by a humorous glance towards her 'friend', who responded with a mimed kiss blown off the palm of his hand.

'We need another chair...' Denis Young announced anxiously.

'Not to worry.' Sally motioned Miss Lubbock to the space on the sofa beside Charlie, dropping down on the arm of it beside her as she settled.

'Well, if that's all right ... Are we ready to begin? What we start with...' Denis turned to the aunt, but shared his gaze with the niece as he stumbled slightly through his explanation of the imminent procedure. 'One of us reads some words of the Enabler, then we each summon – inwardly, of course – our own personal friend from the Other Side' – Phyllida could hear the capital letters – 'and just ... well, just sit in silent contact, gaining strength and reassurance, reminding ourselves – being reminded, I should say – that there's nothing to fear when the time comes for us to cross the Bridge.' A look of embarrassed apology took

96

over the anxious face. 'I'm sorry ... you won't yet have found *your* friends, of course, but we all hope that with the Enabler's help you *will* find them when you come to the meeting next week.' Denis paused for the supportive general murmur.

'You might even,' the mousy-haired girl suggested earnestly, 'discover that the summoning of *our* friends helps you to...' Under a circle of surprised and disapproving glances the soft voice died away.

'Only the Enabler can make the contact,' Charlie boomed disapprovingly. 'He alone mans the Bridge from its earthly end.'

'Am I hearing this?' Sally murmured into Phyllida's ear. Phyllida's own disapproval of this lapse from character was almost neutralized as she saw that on Sally's hitherto unengaged face there was an apparent dawning of attention and interest, so convincing that several of the other attentive faces appeared to be noting it with satisfaction. Miss Lubbock, for her part, maintained the expression of kindly disinterest that Phyllida was discovering was her predominant reaction to her encounters with both the mundane and the bizarre.

'We, of course, know the Enabler's words by heart.' Denis Young paused while he picked up some papers lying on the table beside him. 'But for you ... you may like to read as you listen, and then take the words away with you and read again.' Sally and Phyllida held out their hands to receive the proffered sheets, whereupon Denis Young cleared his throat and began to read from another one, his misplaced emphases and poor breath control contradicting his claim to know the words by heart and giving Phyllida her strongest reaction so far to her first meeting with a collection of Bridgeites, as actress rather than sleuth.

' "You have found your friend; you are safe for ever. When the time comes you will pass from one life to the next with your hand clasped in the hand of one who has made the transition and will draw you safely across the divide. It is right that we cross the Bridge, my beloved ones: we are intended to cross it; but it is a fact as immutable as the fact of eternity that without help many of us fall into the abyss between the worlds and are lost for ever.

' "Why, you will ask, do they fall? Do they fall through wickedness, heedlessness, dimness of spirit? Through lack of love?

' "No, my beloved ones, they fall because they have no one to guide their steps in the shortest, but the most momentous, journey of their lives. Some – I hope many – make the crossing unaided, but without a friend from the other side, reaching out to grasp the beseeching hand, none of us can be certain of our safe arrival into the next world.

98

' "The eternal world? The last and final world? Or simply the next world in a series of worlds we must, as our destiny, traverse? This we do not know, beloved ones; this I cannot tell you. I can only tell you that without your friend you may never discover the ultimate truths, because without your friend you may fall as you seek to cross the Bridge.

' "How do I know this, my beloveds? I know because for some reason that I do not as yet understand I was chosen from the Other Side to be told, to be entrusted with the assurance of eternal safety and decreed by the friend of friends – the first friend to hold out a hand to one of us in this world – to spread the message of certain immortality to every man and woman on this earth.

' "Why now? Why me? My beloveds, this is another question to which I do not as yet have the answer. Our friends on the Other Side, while we are still on earth, have only one answer to only one question: the answer that if we grasp their hand at the moment of death they will guide us across the Bridge. And when we are there with them, when we can thank them and embrace them, it is then, surely, my beloveds, that we will learn the answers to every question that has ever been asked.

' "In the peace of certainty, know you are blessed." '

As he finished reading, Denis Young led

the room in a bowing of heads, and all sat silent, Phyllida suddenly recalling a Quaker meeting she had attended as a teenager, where the silence had been similarly charged. So how simple it had to be, with a flow of purportedly inspirational talk, to electrify the atmosphere where two or three or more were gathered, and make people believe what was good, or what was bad. Or what was downright phoney. Impressed despite herself by the eloquence of the words she had read, if not the words she had heard, Phyllida found with a frisson that she had added the third category as an afterthought, and was relieved when a glance towards Sally was met with a return look that was unambiguously a suppressed grimace; but when Denis Young had cleared his throat again and everyone raised their heads to a general resumption of slight movement, Sally's gaze was guilelessly intense.

'It is impressive, isn't it?' Roma drawled, studying Sally's face.

'Yes.' Sally blinked, and turned to her aunt. 'Oh, yes. I look forward to the experience of meeting your Enabler. Don't you, Auntie?'

'Yes, dear,' Miss Lubbock responded tranquilly. 'I'm sure it will be very interesting.'

'Not *our* Enabler,' Stan shouted, so loudly and unexpectedly that Phyllida's jerk of shock was barely contained inside Miss

100

Lubbock's tweed jacket. Stan's twitchings had continued throughout the reading, and during the ensuing silence, but this was the first time he had used his voice. 'Everyone's.'

'I'm sorry,' Sally responded promptly, turning to face him. 'Please forgive me. I didn't mean to sound disrespectful. Just put it down to ignorance.'

Only Roma, Phyllida observed, appeared to have picked up – and even appreciated – the possibility of a gentle teasing in Sally's apology. Her mouth twitched and her eyes flickered, but everyone else was nodding vigorously and murmuring absolution with serious faces.

'You'll learn,' Denis assured the two newcomers, 'and when you hear the words in the mouth of the Enabler himself, you'll learn quickly. Now, we have tea or coffee at this point. Which would you like?'

Both Phyllida and Sally chose coffee, and Denis reminded Tom and Felicity that it was their turn to make the drinks. They were a totally unexceptional pair, Phyllida thought as she watched them lag towards the door hand in hand – no distinguishing features beyond the identical absorbed looks they were exchanging; not tall or short, fat or thin, attractive or repellent. The impression was confirmed as they paused in the doorway and asked in a coincidence of flat voices if Miss Lubbock and Sally wanted milk and/or sugar.

'They've been transformed,' Denis informed his visitors enthusiastically, dragging his chair across to the sofa without getting up from it.

'Ah yes,' Miss Lubbock responded. 'Will they be getting married soon?'

'By the Enabler,' Denis corrected her, with a touch of severity. 'They are our newest members, still in the glow of discovery.'

'Were they engaged when they joined you?' Sally asked.

'I don't know. I suppose so.' Impatience, now. Their engagement, Denis was implying, was irrelevant in the light of the larger revelation, and Phyllida hoped she might just have learned that the Enabler did not control an additional bridge connecting – or dividing – people who were both still in this world. 'They've been lucky, I suppose,' he added grudgingly, 'finding each other as well as their friends on the Other Side.'

'You haven't found *your* friend on *this* side yet, Denis?' – Sally, openly teasing now.

'No.' There had been an involuntary glance at Sam, which it was obvious the reddening Denis immediately regretted.

'I'm sure you will,' Sally encouraged him. 'I've found mine, and it's wonderful. You'll know when it happens.' She had raised her voice slightly, and gained the general attention, which even before she spoke had been biased towards the newcomers.

'Too much fuss about togetherness.' Charlie jerked irritably in her half of the sofa, making Phyllida bounce slightly. 'You can't escape it anywhere – supermarket check-out, magazine racks, even the quality newspapers these days. You're not complete unless you're a duo. Rubbish!'

So whatever Charlie's sexual persuasion, she did not see it in terms of permanence. Sally had leaned towards Samantha.

'I've been trying to think where I've seen you before. I think it was outside Billing station, handing things out. Am I right?'

'Yes. This past week I've—'

'Perhaps we shall be able to entrust *you*, Sally, with spreading the word when you've heard the Enabler!' The brief sprightliness fell away from Denis as he looked round the room, sighing. 'I do so wish he would come here; the place would be for ever blessed.'

'Nothing would ever bless *this* room,' Sally breathed. Denis Young had overlaid the anonymity of Miss Lubbock's living room with baleful-looking zodiacal throws, unconvincing plastic flowers, esoterically apocalyptic posters – some with peeling corners – and a strong smell of joss sticks.

'Well,' Miss Lubbock said, 'if the Enabler *did* come here, Denis, you'd feel then that you could never leave Pickford Heights, and

103

you told me the other morning that you'd like to.'

'You're a regular Pollyanna, Auntie!' Sally caught Sam's eye as she laughed, and to her and Phyllida's pleasure Sam laughed too, looking so bright and beautiful Phyllida felt a pang of sorrow for the Chief Superintendent's sister, denied any share in her daughter's joys.

Trays of tea and coffee and two plates of rather boring biscuits were brought in as the laughter died, and for the next half-hour, as it was slowly drunk and the biscuits eaten, the desultory chat was the sort of thing that would have been heard in any gathering of young men and women, except that awareness of the Enabler's promises was woven into the exchanges so regularly and seamlessly Phyllida found herself awed by the seriousness of the man's skills – and that she was looking forward to the Barton Street meeting more keenly and curiously than she had looked forward to anything since Jack had died.

Seven

'Hello!' Denis Young again, this time standing in the dingy doorway of the old De Luxe cinema, smiling triumphantly and reminding Phyllida of a dog who has just spotted the master he was half-afraid he might have lost; and the slight trembling of his body made her think irresistibly of the wagging of a docked tail.

'Good evening, Denis. I hope we're not late?'

'You're early, actually.' Thus saving him moments of the anxiety Phyllida had seen in his eyes as she and Sally approached him. 'Let me find you seats.'

'Not too near the front, please,' Miss Lubbock decreed as they entered the small lobby. 'We're here to observe, you know,' Phyllida added truthfully. 'You can't measure in advance the kind of effect charisma will have on the individual members of an audience, and life has taught me to be something of a cynic.'

'I understand,' Denis responded, his enthusiasm undimmed; 'but when you hear ...

and Sally ... I can't believe you're a cynic, Sally.'

'I'm not sure what I am,' Sally said brightly, 'but I hope I have an open mind. And whatever Auntie says about herself, she still has one, too.'

'Good, good.' They had moved into the larger area with its short rows of sagging seats, which Denis was surveying with a wisp of doubt in his face like a cirrus cloud across a blue sky. 'I'm afraid it's a bit grotty, but it's cleaner than it looks – we all see to that – and Mr Dixon has plans ... How about here? Just about halfway and on the aisle so that you can put your legs—'

'Mr Dixon?' Sally had moved in to the farther of the indicated seats, and Phyllida turned to Denis as she edged Miss Lubbock's padding in front of the nearer.

'The Bridge's business manager – and the Enabler's right-hand man. Mr Dixon looks after the ... well, the practicalities: arrangements and timetables and so on, as well as the finances – so that our leader is freed from the ... well, from the headaches of the everyday running of ... well, not the business, of course, but what any organization needs to take care of if it's to flourish in other ways as well as in the spiritual. I mean...'

'Of course.' Miss Lubbock sank into her seat with a beam of smile. 'Thank you for

106

your attention, Denis; we both appreciate it. But now you must go and look after other people as well, as it appears you're on duty. We'll be all right.'

'We will, you know,' Sally assured him, as his suddenly anxious gaze shifted to her, and remained there. 'We'll see you later.'

'Of course. Perhaps even...' Hope gleamed through. 'When we all get back to the Heights you might feel you could join me for coffee or cocoa and we can talk about ... well, about what the meeting has done for you.'

'Thank you.' Miss Lubbock smiled again. 'But I suspect I shall be too tired, especially if I experience what you're hoping I will. And Sally's boyfriend tends to drop in to say goodnight.'

'Ah.' The buoyancy of the mood engendered by the imminent performance of the Enabler almost held disappointment at bay. 'Of course. But if you're not too ... overcome ... you'd be very welcome on your own, Miss Lubbock, if ... if Sally can't make it.'

'Thank you,' Miss Lubbock repeated. 'Anyway, I expect some of your young friends will be going back with you for a nightcap?'

'Well ... I don't really think so. It's ... well, it's sort of draining; it's so wonderful, we tend to go our ways at the end. But it would be great if you feel you could...'

'We'll see'; but Phyllida already knew that duty would not take her as far as a late-night private showing of Denis Young's post-meeting euphoria. 'Off you go now, Denis,' Miss Lubbock pursued, as firmly as she ever spoke. 'And be a good steward.'

'Ah, yes. Of course. Ha, ha!' – and he was at last on his way, bumping into a couple of people as he moved off backwards, his eyes on Sally.

Some of the young people they had met in his flat came past them, but they had clearly started to concentrate on the spiritual experience to come and those who noticed and recognized Miss Lubbock and niece did no more than smile and nod or offer a brief greeting, leaving Phyllida and Sally free to look around them.

Steve's comparison with the audience at the nude shows in the old Windmill Theatre had been apt: anoraks, now, rather than raincoats, and women as well as men, but those who were not among the minority who seemed to be already rapt with anticipation looked wary and hesitant, eyes down, settling quickly into their seats, clearly hoping not to run into a friend or acquaintance who had succumbed as they had to the insidious appeal of the leaflet that had been thrust into their hands.

The dim art deco lights on walls and

ceiling – their glass shades orange-brown still from the cigarette-smoke coating of years – had, Phyllida suspected, been left uncleaned to encourage those who would rather not be seen to have been netted by The Bridge propaganda; a revealing glare of illumination could have had the more tentative souls turning the entrance into the exit within seconds.

'More young than old,' Sally murmured, as four giggling girls settled into the seats in front of them.

'But quite a few of the mature, dear.' It was Miss Lubbock's slow voice that answered. 'And something of an atmosphere, one must concede.' Whether generated by the cognoscenti or by anticipation of the revelatory unknown it was as yet impossible to say, but there was no doubting the buzz of excitement around them, and that it was growing. And the spaces were filling up. When Phyllida and Sally had arrived, there had been isolated small groups and lone figures, but these were perforce being linked as more people arrived; and all the time the young ones they had already met were moving about with their unvarying contented smiles, their eyes, even when they greeted people, seeming to look inwards. Her own eyes predominantly on Samantha Mason through the gloom, Phyllida felt another pang of pity for her family.

'What is it?' Sally had shivered.

'I don't know. It suddenly feels a bit scary. I mean ... one man without any tradition of religious belief to back him up, bringing all these people here, making this atmosphere...'

'I know. And I know from having had that glimpse of him when I went to his home that he's ... unusual.'

'But you said it was his stillness.'

'It was. So perhaps that's the other side of the same coin.'

'And no props. Ah...' Sally laughed a little shrilly as some New Age music began to drift out from behind the narrow, curtained stage.

'Music's powerful. I'm not surprised. The already faithful obviously don't need it, but for the merely curious ... Here we go, Sally.'

The curtains, their lower folds illumined dramatically from beneath by lights that had probably been the signal for the magic to begin years ago on the screen behind them, were slowly parting. No screen now, just a small space with a battered upright piano to one side, three chairs in a row and a couple of tubular-legged tables, one to the side of the chairs with a vase of lilies upon it, the other carrying a carafe of water and a glass and placed closest to the central of the chairs – the Masonic throne of Steve's report.

'The Enabler's chair, the Enabler's wife's, and Mr Dixon's.'

The hissed whisper made Phyllida jump, but it was only Denis, pausing beside them on his way forward.

'Thank you. Does Mrs ... Does the Enabler's wife play a part?'

'Oh, no. Nobody else does.'

A slight reproof, perhaps, and Denis had moved on – was slipping into an aisle seat in the third row, just as the clapping began.

It reminded Phyllida of those past news films of the Russian praesidium in session, sitting in solemn rows clapping an empty rostrum; and a goose walked over her grave. It was with the remembered reassurance of Steve's triumphant immunity that she looked up at the beam of light steadily concentrating on to the centre of the three chairs, and waited as the clapping swelled and nothing and no one appeared to inspire the crescendo, although the two young people on duty were standing one each side of the stage at the top of the short flights of steps up to it, their hands busy and their faces rapt.

When the applause could rise no higher, the illuminated back drape was drawn aside and a figure advanced slowly to the edge of the stage, a figure for which Phyllida and Sally were prepared, but which evoked a low hiss of surprise and disappointment from

111

other newcomers to a Bridge meeting: a small man with neat, grey hair and a conventional grey suit, grey-complexioned and solemn-faced, without a gesture to offer – even his hands hung at his sides, and remained there as he paused at the centre front of the stage, waiting for the rapid dying of the applause to be complete.

'Friends,' he said then, in a voice richer and more powerful than his appearance had suggested. 'Welcome to this meeting of The Bridge. Before our Enabler appears to inspire us, I as business manager have a few notices to give out. Our next open meeting will be at this same time, half past seven, here at the De Luxe four weeks from today, the twenty-seventh of April. Roma Westlake and Colin Heard will be on main duty' – confirmation, perhaps, with the working presence that evening of Tom and Felicity, the engaged couple encountered at Denis's flat, that The Bridge did not seek to sever earthly bonds. 'Meetings of the Finance and PR committees will take place here as usual during the coming month'; and at some point in the evening, Phyllida reflected, finance would be sought from this audience. Probably unannounced, to lessen the likelihood of a creeping exodus under cover of the darkness beyond the bright circle of the spotlight. 'But I have the happy duty now to announce an unprecedented event: our

Enabler is offering the hospitality of his home to all who have pledged a regular financial contribution to The Bridge, and to those of their families and friends who are here tonight and have a sincere interest in his message. The hospitality is to be offered on Sunday next from eleven a.m. until four p.m. at the Enabler's country home, and our members will be given the address and the route out of Seaminster. Please join me now in expressing our appreciation to the Enabler and Mrs Henderson for their generous gesture.' The voice that was drowned by applause had ended on as uninflected a note as it had begun. Perhaps, Phyllida thought, to ensure that no comparison could be made with the oratory to come.

As the applause died, the two standing young people descended to their seats in the auditorium and Mr Dixon walked slowly back to the chairs. In front of the one to the right of the throne he turned and, with the only gesture he had yet displayed, flung out an arm to the back of the stage before inaugurating another burst of Soviet-style applause.

Sally was wriggling in her seat and Phyllida could feel a tingle in her spine as the back drape was again drawn aside and a second man stepped on to the stage, arms outstretched. One of them dipped momentarily on to his manager's shoulder as he

113

advanced past him to the front of the stage, where he held them stretched forward for a few seconds as the applause crescendoed, before gesturing that it should cease. As it obediently did so, he raised them again towards the audience, and began to speak.

'My dear, dear people. I am here with a very simple message: when you have found your friend on the Other Side, you will be safe for ever...'

The words were pretty much what Denis Young had read out, but their delivery, and the impact of the man who was now expressing them, loaded them with an insistence to attention before which even Phyllida's alerted agnosticism was for a few moments in abeyance.

'There is a friend for each and every one of you, waiting to clasp your hand and, when the time comes, help you safely across the divide. My dear, dear people, I know this for the truth of truths. My own friend has told me, told me as clearly as I tell you now, and I believe what I hear him say. And should I waver, should even I wonder in my human pessimism how something so wonderful can be true, he will tell me again, and again, whenever I ask him...'

Yes, it was the other side of the stillness she had witnessed on the man's stately terrace, although the stillness was still there behind the gestures of the arms, the movements in the face, the trembling of the body, in some indefinable way intensifying them. And helped hugely, if not entirely – Phyllida's scepticism was thankfully reasserting itself – by the physical blessings nature had bestowed upon the man: height, lean strength, large, beautiful hands, a voice that was song in speech, thick, grey hair, huge eyes and fine but strong features in a face that showed the structure of its bones. There were fleeting similarities to the sister Phyllida had encountered in the family chapel, which reminded her that Hermione Henderson did not appear to be part of her brother's audience – not that her presence was to be expected, given her derisive description of The Bridge. Nevertheless, Phyllida diverted her now less than rapt gaze to the chairs behind the Enabler to confirm the absence of his sister, and saw for the first time that his wife, who must have entered behind him unnoticed in the razzmatazz of his reception, was sitting the other side of the throne from his business manager, gazing up at her husband's back. The chairs were on the edge of the spotlight's brilliant circle, and it was impossible to make out if Mrs Henderson was wearing any more facial expression than Mr Dixon had so far displayed; but as the Enabler's performance continued, Phyllida could see that both her glance and her stance – very upright and leaning slightly forward – remained steady until the Enabler finally dropped his arms to his sides, bent his head, and walked backwards to his throne as the applause once more swelled, touching its edge with the back of his knees without turning round – rehearsal had surely been necessary – before sitting down and placing his hands on its carved knobs, head still bowed. Then Mrs Henderson showed her profile, as for a brief moment she turned towards him.

It was Mr Dixon now who rose and gestured the audience to silence, whereupon the Enabler got to his feet again but did not move away from his chair. 'We do not call it prayer,' he said, his charisma, Phyllida thought, even more compelling for being muted; 'we call it contact. I will now contact my own friend. Not for my own reassurance, but to ask him to help join those around him individually with those here in this audience who have not yet discovered – have not, perhaps, begun to seek – their own personal friend. That friend who, once found, will be with them constantly to assure them of that everlasting life into which they will be conducted when the time comes for them to leave this world and enter the next. The next, my dear people, but not perhaps the last. Unlike the religions of history, which have given rise to so much misery in their insistence that they hold the secret of the nature of eternity and must impose it on others, members of The Bridge know no more than that the beginnings of eternity are to be found immediately following earthly death, and that the friend made on the other side will ensure safe passage into it. Be with me now, my dear, dear people' – voice, gestures, intensity swelling to full strength – 'and you will find your friend on the other side, the friend who will enter your spirit and be there throughout your life and into your death. Make contact now.'

The Enabler bowed his head, and for a few moments following the slight flurry engendered by his audience following suit, there was no sound anywhere in the auditorium. Phyllida was again reminded of the Quaker meeting she had long ago attended, the silence was so potent – not as warmly as it had been among the other Friends, where a few gentle souls had conducted that meeting unintrusively into its silence. Now, Phyllida found the Enabler's lead had made her wary and defensive as she caught herself wondering how she would feel if she suddenly believed that what he had told his audience was true...

Jack ... If I could know for certain that you had me by the hand...

No! Not this way! I do know. I don't need this

117

man, or any other, to tell me...

One of the girls in front of her had gasped, then squealed; then shouted out, 'Oh, Gawd!'

The spotlight had dimmed, but Phyllida saw the Enabler raise his head and nod, as two of the young members of The Bridge came racing up the aisle to encourage the affected one out into it – fortunately her seat was close to the end of the row – where they embraced the trembling girl and held her upright.

'It's good,' Phyllida heard. 'It's very good ... What's your name?'

'V-Vera!'

'It's very good, Vera. Don't be afraid. You've been blessed. Write your name, address and telephone number on this slip' – a small white oblong changed hands – 'and one of us will be in touch with you and welcome you into the circle of the blessed.' Surely a designated form of words, not something off the top of Roma's head – not that Phyllida thought this particular young member of The Bridge wasn't clever enough to have improvised; she just felt that, un-brainwashed by the Enabler, Roma's native sense of irony would have made her incapable of giving voice to them.

A gulp and mumbled thanks, and Vera was stumbling back into her seat. No voice disturbed the subsequent moments of silence, though Phyllida thought she heard a couple of groans and some of the heads in front of her were swaying. Sally, to her relief, remained still, until a slight movement made her turn her own head sharply towards her, where to her relief she met dancing-eyed amusement.

It was a relief, too, that the spotlight brightened and the house lights came on without further incident, although Phyllida's reaction was tempered by an unwelcome suspicion that she was even more relieved at having ... what? Managed to escape something there had been a moment's danger might have caught her? Whatever, she had not been caught, nor had Sally; but Samantha Mason could have uttered a cry that would have pierced her mother's heart and lowered the dark brows of her Uncle Maurice...

The atmosphere had eased, and Mr Dixon was on his feet again, inviting the audience to ask the Enabler questions. Phyllida saw this as brave, until she remembered Steve's suspicion that the questioners and questions had been decided in advance – which couldn't, though, exclude the possibility of a sceptic intervening.

The questions, however, were all respectful, and met by the Enabler without pause. Did one know whether one's friend was male or female? Yes, one got a sense of male or female, but it wasn't important. Did men find men friends, and women find women? Not necessarily. How did you know when you had found him or her? This revelation, the Enabler regretted, could not be put into words, but when you did find him or her, you would not need to ask that question. Say you found your friend when you were young and lived to a ripe old age, would he or she still be around? Of course, and – here there was a moment of severity – it would be very wrong, and a betrayal of all trust, as well as totally unnecessary, to cut one's earthly life short by one's own hand in order to ensure one's friend's abiding loyalty.

That was a reassurance for the Kendrick clan that Phyllida wrote down word for word under cover of the grudging lights.

After half an hour the Enabler drew a dramatic hand across his fine forehead, and the watchful Mr Dixon got to his feet to announce the end of the question-and-answer session. As he spoke, young people jumped to their feet and started handing single sheets along the rows, the large-print words of what to Steve had 'sounded like a hymn'. At the same time an elderly woman made heavy weather up one of the sets of steps and sank down on the piano stool. The words were a loosely metric version of the crux of the Enabler's sermon, sung to a tune almost familiar to Phyllida from childhood

120

church attendances, and the lead of the strong young voices was quickly taken up by the rest of the audience.

We blissfully acknowledge
The shining path ahead,
The certainty that we shall never
Never
Fall among the dead...

'A bit all-right-Jack,' Sally murmured, 'but hardly subversive.'

'And hardly poetry, alas.'

As the music died away the Enabler got to his feet again and wished everyone the discovery of a friend before administering what sounded like a form of blessing – 'May your friend be with you, tonight and for always' – before leaving the stage. Mr Dixon recapped his notices, adding that a collection would be taken at the doors, where forms of membership would be available for people to take away with them.

Neither Phyllida nor Sally was surprised to see a line of young people smilingly obstructing the exit, but no one was attempting to circumvent them, even though the shallowness of the bowl each was holding meant that donations of copper demanded more nerve than any members of the departing audience appeared to possess.

'Shaken, if not stirred,' was Sally's mur-

121

mured judgement on their morale, and Phyllida agreed with her, except in the case of the suggestible Vera, who was still being supported by her slightly abashed peers.

'How was it for you?' Another hiss into her ear, and this time Phyllida identified it without looking round: only Denis Young would put anyone so crassly on the spot.

'Interesting, Denis,' Miss Lubbock responded. 'Very interesting.'

'Sally?' The dog really could have done with its tail.

'Yes. Interesting. Very.'

'You felt something?'

'Oh, yes. Although at the moment I can't define it.'

Phyllida wondered if Sally might ever be persuaded to work officially for the Agency.

'Ah! That's good.'

'May we give you a lift home in our taxi, Denis?' Phyllida asked, remembering the Enabler's open day. 'Sally's about to ring for one.'

'Ah,' came again, this time dispiritedly. 'I'm afraid I have my car. I'd run you both home, of course, but I'm afraid I'm on duty here for a bit longer so I can't...'

'Of course not. And I think we're both a bit – well, overcome, for a talking session tonight. In fact Sally's going to ring her boyfriend and tell him not to come round as she wants to go straight to bed.'

'Of course. But you'll come to another meeting?'

'I'm sure we shall.' Phyllida thought gratefully of the sanctuary of the Golden Lion, from which eventually Miss Lubbock would fail to emerge.

'Great. And in the meantime ... could I invite you both to the open day at the Enabler's home? It would be wonderful if you felt you could come. I mean ... you're both sincerely interested following this evening, aren't you? Sally?'

'We are, and we'd love to come, wouldn't we, Auntie?'

'Yes, dear.'

'Gosh, that's great. I'm afraid I shan't be able to give you a lift, though; I've got to be—'

'On duty. Don't worry, Denis, Sally will drive us. We'll just need directions.'

'Of course. I'll put them through your letter box tomorrow, so that you'll have lots of time to study them. Next Sunday, then ... Hi, Sam. I'm just coming.'

Denis's gaze wandered uncertainly between the two blonde beauties. Sally was smiling in a relaxed way, but Samantha was frowning. 'The Enabler's asking for you, Denis. You don't keep the Enabler waiting.'

As they emerged into the street, Sally's mobile at her ear and Steve staring at them morosely from the window of the chippy, the brief euphoria of Phyllida's mood was shattered by the reminder in Samantha Mason's gimlet-eyed face that all she had achieved to date was information, and that as far as the Kendrick family was concerned there was still the whole way to go.

Eight

He felt good when he set out, and better and better as he swung along the cliff path. Gulls were wheeling and crying over the edge of the tide, which was breaking very gently on the sand, turning matt to gloss as it slowly retreated before its next, and closer, encroachment. Everything around him seemed astonishingly beautiful, and he was seeing it with a clarity he had never experienced before, every least detail brilliantly glittering: the swooping birds, the blue sky with its wisps of thin cloud, the high, hazy sun slightly warm on his face, the sand and the creaming water's edge so far below him. It was as if he was seeing it all for the first time; but he was, of course, seeing it for the last time, bathed in a valedictory glow.

He had no fear. What he was about to do

was inevitable – logical. Bliss awaited him; his hand was already in his friend's grasp. Yes, he was sad to be saying goodbye to the places he so loved, to the health and strength of his body as it flowed along; but how much better to lose it while it *was* strong and healthy, to lose the beauty around him while his eyes were clear and bright to see it! To cross the Bridge in bliss!

'I am coming,' he whispered; and then, because he was alone and there would be no one to hold him back, 'I am coming!' he shouted, twirling on the spot in his excitement, an excitement more intense than any he had ever felt before, tingling through him and culminating in the throbbing warmth of his right hand which was being so masterfully held.

At the green edge of the cliff, when the last of the cottages above it was out of sight, his friend lifted their hands aloft, and he raised his other hand too as he yelled 'Goodbye!' Then, on a last giddy image of sand, sea and sky, he leapt into space.

'I saw him!' the girl sobbed. 'I shouted, but he didn't hear, or if he did, he didn't take any notice. He was waving his arms about and then ... then he just jumped. I couldn't make myself go and look and anyway I knew he'd have to be dead, so I just sat down here on the grass with my mobile and ... and...'

'You acted by the book,' the WPC said soothingly, shifting her aching thighs as she remained reluctantly crouched beside the weeping girl. 'Had you seen him before? Have you any idea who he was?'

Shouts from the beach came thinly up to them, but the girl had made her call well away from the cliff edge, and all that could be seen from the grassy slope where she sat hugging her knees was the gently heaving expanse of blue-green sea to the distant horizon.

'Oh, God. They've found him.'

'They will have done ... Betty, isn't it? Betty Bennett? Have you any idea who the man was?'

'No. I mean, I was a bit of a way off, but I'm sure I'd have recognized someone I knew, and I'd never seen this chap before.'

'Before he jumped ... apart from waving his arms, was he behaving in any other way that made you particularly notice him? Made you afraid he might do something ... dangerous?'

'Not something dangerous, but he *was* sort of dancing along. I suppose that was why I was watching him. He turned round a couple of times, sort of staring at the sky, and I did feel sort of vaguely that he was a bit close to the edge to be doing that. But I never thought ... Oh, God!' The tears began to flow again, and for her own comfort as

126

much as for the comfort of the unhappy witness, WPC Graham eased her backside to the ground and put an arm across the girl's heaving shoulders.

'It's all right, Betty, it's all right. There was nothing you could do beyond what you did. You mustn't let what you've seen prey on your mind. We'll get some counselling set up to help you cope.'

Kendrick was away from the station until late afternoon, on business with the Chief Constable, and the first event of his return was the arrival of DS Fred Wetherhead in his private office.

'A young chappie threw himself over the west cliff a couple of hours ago,' Wetherhead said, dropping his short, heavy body into the chair the DCS had nodded towards. 'Name of Stan Dolby. I think you're going to be interested in him, sir. The uniforms involved were having a late nosh just now, and so was I – Barnacle Bill took longer to sober up this morning than usual. I was at the next table and hardly listening, but I caught the word "Bridge" and then I was all ears.' Fred Wetherhead smiled ruefully as Kendrick jerked in his seat. 'In fact I joined in their chat and told 'em casually that I'd been handed a leaflet with that word on it the other night by a youngster outside the station, and that it had appeared to me to be a wrapped-up message about making death seem attractive. Then the WPC said yes! When she saw the leaflet that was in the suicide's pocket it had seemed familiar and she'd thought she must have seen a copy lying around somewhere. I suggested the copy found on the suicide ought to be investigated. It's bagged up anyway, of course, and on its way to Forensics, but I don't reckon that need stop you, or your, your...'

'My private contact from making that investigation. I expect – well, I hope, Fred – that the contact has met this unfortunate fellow and can tell me something about him.'

'But it's still not a police matter?'

Kendrick sighed, and swivelled his chair round for the solace of the huge marine view spread out beyond his window and the police car park. 'There's no doubt whatsoever that the man was on his own when he jumped?'

'None, if we believe what the apparently one and only witness has told us. Young girl. And her story of having just left the cottage nearest to the spot, after lunching with some friends who live there, has been confirmed by the extended family who were entertaining her ... You're worrying about your niece, aren't you, sir?'

'No point in worrying about the chap who

jumped.' Kendrick swung his chair back to his desk, and the concerned, kindly face of his favourite subordinate. 'Yes, of course I am. If that's what this brainwashing can do...'

'The chap who died could have a history of instability,' Wetherhead suggested. 'That's always the type that's vulnerable to demagogues. Your niece doesn't sound in the least—'

'None of us knows my niece very well these days, Fred; but I hope to God you're right. Get me the gen on the suicide's background as quickly as you can. Not that I can delay a call to my sister, because I can't stop tonight's news giving the chap's name, although I want the Bridge connection withheld from the media for the time being.'

'Of course, sir.'

For a moment, master and man surveyed one another without expression, although Kendrick was pretty certain his sergeant was asking the same mental question as he was asking himself: would he have decreed the embargo if his niece hadn't been a member of the sect both policemen knew was responsible, however innocently, for a death?

'Thank you, Fred. Was the body carrying evidence of the man's identity?'

'Yes. Stanley Dolby. I got the name from the uniforms as casually as I could. He's local.'

'Well done.' And Phyllida Moon could have met him.

When DS Wetherhead had left, Kendrick's first call was to the Peter Piper Agency.

'Is she with you, Peter?'

'Miss Bowden's with a client. Urgent enough, I suspect, for me to interrupt them.'

'I'm sorry, but if you would.' He had no call to feel impatient during the two-minute wait for Phyllida Moon, but of course he did, although he tried to subdue the unjustified sensation.

'Maurice?' It was her own voice, and it calmed him.

'Yes. Phyllida, have you met a character called Stanley Dolby?'

'I have. The only youngster at Denis Young's evening who looked less – or more – than ordinary. Staring into space and twitching, and not appearing to make eye contact with anyone. Is that a help?'

'My very dear girl, it is. Particularly for Maurice and Mary Kendrick.' Kendrick coughed, as introduction to comparative formality: 'Dolby threw himself over the cliff earlier today, on the way west past where the listed cottages finish. There was a witness, who said he was alone and waving his arms about before he jumped.'

He heard the shocked intake of breath.

130

'I'm so sorry, but I'm not vastly surprised. So it has to be suicide?'

'Unless a young girl or a member of the family she'd been lunching with pushed him over. And thank God it isn't realistic to consider *that*. You feel it could have been in character, then?'

'I feel – I felt – as soon as I saw Stan Dolby that he wasn't as other people, that he was seeing distant visions rather than what was going on around him. In fact he made me think of his master, the time I saw Henderson on his stately terrace staring into space. Their eccentricities were somehow alike, even though at the time one was still and the other one was throwing himself about. You know from my report, and Steve's, now, that the master throws himself about too.' Phyllida hesitated. 'Maurice, do impress upon your sister that Dolby was ... different, that what he did mustn't make her afraid for her daughter.'

'Thank you.' How had he ever managed to feel grudging towards this woman? 'It'll help when I break the news.' The formality had gone again, and he wasn't going to bring it back. 'But with parents...'

'Something I can only imagine. Really, though – Stan Dolby was weird.' Phyllida hesitated again, giving Kendrick a chance to speak, which he didn't take. 'Maurice, you'd like me to get Samantha's reaction as soon

131

as possible – and the reactions of the other young Bridgeites?'

'I was getting round to asking you. Thanks. You chose the Emily Lubbock character well: it's surely in her nature, when she hears the news, to hasten along the corridor.'

'Of course. And with a shocked Sally in tow. It'll be a help if the news breaks in the media before we set off.'

'It will. With the exception of the Bridge connection. But if none of them is watching or listening...'

'I know.' Phyllida smiled at Peter across his desk. 'Miss Lubbock will have to tell them. Oh, while we're speaking: Steve followed Henderson and Dixon when they left Barton Street last night, and they both went back to Fifield Place.'

'He followed them all the way?'

'Far enough, we gather, to be pretty certain where they were making for, together.'

'Thank you. That was devotion to duty, if with a negative result. Now back to your client, Miss Bowden.'

Recruiting Sally for the evening wasn't difficult, but Phyllida had to remind her with a touch of severity that her wig – as it always would be when not being worn – was in the small bedroom at the Golden Lion and that she must leave the hotel already a blonde. 'I'll ring Reception now and tell them to expect you and let you into my office. Seeing a brunette arrive and a blonde leave is par for their course, so just walk out with a smile. If we're lucky, Sally, someone among the young Bridge troops will have seen or heard the news. But it'll still take a while for them to be rallied and Miss Lubbock and her niece can really only call on Denis once, so we'll make ourselves wait until after the late-evening news, and hope that the rally won't be taking place else-where – and that the lad won't be on his own, sniffing his joss sticks in blissful ignor-ance. Either way, if we don't find him at home there's always tomorrow.'

'I know'; but Phyllida had heard the gusty sigh. 'So how about if your blonde sidekick brings in a couple of pizzas? You won't want to be bothered with cooking.'

'I never do. But tonight especially not. So yes, that would be great. Thanks. I'll let you eat yours as a brunette.'

'So you won't be ... Phyllida, could I watch you transform?'

Phyllida found herself laughing. 'If you'd like to. No one ever has, now I think about it. Or expressed a wish to.'

'Because I'm the only assistant you've ever had. Thanks, I'll be fascinated. I'll just sit quietly, but if you find me a distraction I'll leave you to it.'

'I shan't, I'll be in my groove. But Sally ...

don't get your hopes up: it could be a waste of time for both of us. I'll have to transform before we contact Denis, and when we do we could find he's gone out, not knowing what's happened or sharing his sorrows elsewhere.'

'I know, your poor skin ... But even if he's home alone, we'll get *something*.'

'Sally, if you ever fancy a change of career, I think I can vouch for Peter that the Agency could find it has a vacancy.'

'Gosh! I can't believe—' Voices in the background made Sally break off, and when she resumed she sounded rueful. 'That was my current career reminding me that I'm ambitious as a librarian.'

'And Jeremy would remind you that private investigating is a dangerous occupation.'

'Phooey to him if he does ... Anyway, even if I decide I've got to carry on as a librarian and not waste the exams I've taken so far, I'm going to indulge myself in some fabulous imagining ... and I'm going to enjoy the rest of *this* operation!'

'I'm not sure "enjoy" is the right word, but I'm fairly certain it'll carry on being interesting.'

The suicide on the south coast was the last item on the early-evening national television news, and the first on the immediately following local bulletin. The national item was a bald announcement of the death, unillustrated, but the local item was fuller and given against dramatic pictures of the area that played up the long face of the cliff and the jagged rocks at the foot of it.

The victim was a local man, Stanley Dolby, 27.

'They give your age,' Sally whispered, wriggling in her seat, 'whatever else they leave out. Always.'

Mr Dolby lived alone in Seaminster, and had not appeared to be in any way distressed.

'Any more than normal,' commented Sally. This time Phyllida shushed her.

An eyewitness confirms that Mr Dolby was alone on the cliff edge when he jumped, and foul play is not suspected. Now here's Anthea with the local weather.

So Maurice had managed to keep the Bridge connection out of it.

'It doesn't mention his connection with The Bridge.'

'Probably the police don't know about it.'

'But if and when they find out ... it won't do The Bridge any good. Incitement to suicide, or something? That'd make our investigation really difficult, if not impossible, because the Enabler and Co. would go all defensive.'

'So let's hope the connection isn't made.' *Let's hope what the Chief of Police will be hoping.*

The pizzas were good, but Sally un-characteristically failed to clean her plate, and relaxed only when she had settled into the chair she had pulled into a corner of Phyllida's bedroom. Despite her assurance that a spectator wouldn't worry her, Phyllida had been slightly afraid that it would, but in the event she soon forgot Sally, remembering her only when she had finally sat down at what passed for a dressing table in standard Heights furniture, and saw her in the mirror behind her own image, leaning forward with flushed, absorbed face, her hands between her denim knees.

'You may find this the best bit,' Phyllida said, smiling past her pictured head. 'I'm got up as Emily Lubbock, and now I'm going to become her.'

'Gosh...' Sally had thought Phyllida was already that plump elderly lady, but as she studied the face in the mirror and saw it subtly but steadily change, she realized that it had still been Phyllida who had just spoken to her.

'Right you are, dear.' Miss Lubbock rose from the rickety stool and turned to smile at her niece. 'I think it's time you went and got yourself ready, too.' She consulted the watch on a wrist that somehow, to Sally, looked less slender and attractive than it had looked half an hour or so earlier. 'The second news

136

carrying the death will soon be over, and that's the one Miss Lubbock and her niece have seen. I'll ring Denis in ten minutes or so, and then with luck we'll be invited over.'

They had the luck. Phyllida knew from Denis's sepulchral monosyllable that he had heard the dreadful news, and she could hear agitated murmurs behind him.

'It's Miss Lubbock, Denis. Sally and I have just seen the news ... Oh, my dear, we're so very sorry. If there's anything we can do...'

Two hands were raised simultaneously aloft, fingers crossed, and for an unnerving moment Phyllida had to subdue an inward giggle that threatened to erupt.

'I don't think anyone can do anything. But if you'd like to join us, share our mourning, well, you'd both be very welcome.'

'Thank you, Denis. But we don't want to intrude...' *Reculer pour mieux sauter.* It was a gamble that felt familiar.

'You wouldn't be. Really. So do come and comfort us.'

'Very well.' Phyllida nodded her satisfaction, and Sally spread her hands across her face, staring wide-eyed over them. 'Now?'

'Yes, come now. We've tea and coffee going.'

The smell of incense was very strong in Denis's narrow hall, but Phyllida found it preferable to the odour of stale vegetables that had prevailed on their last visit. His cronies were draped around his sitting room in much the same attitudes as when Phyllida and Sally had first seen them, but – with the exception, Phyllida quickly noticed, of Roma and Colin – their facial expressions were very different: no more dreamy evidence of the mental drug that had brought them together. The engaged couple, still in their corner, were clinging together, Tom stroking Felicity's hair; mousy Marian had red eyes and a trembling mouth, and Samantha Mason looked wide-eyed and imploring, with a glint of tears on her cheeks. Even big Charlie's hostile glance was half-obscured by a large handkerchief. Denis, Phyllida thought, was trying, without entire success, to subdue a sense of excitement under a cloak of solemnity.

'So here we all are,' he announced pompously: 'together, but never again to be complete.'

Sam gave a hiccuping sob, and Phyllida felt another stab of pity for Maurice Kendrick's sister – and of anger against the man who for a brief instant had penetrated her own defences: people who could stir strong facile emotions were hideously dangerous when they chose to exercise their powers irresponsibly. Remembering her evening in the De Luxe cinema, Phyllida found herself suddenly surprised that this was the first –

at least, the first recorded – casualty of the Enabler's heady message. When she had first met these young people she had hoped for Kendrick's sake, and for her own sense of apprehensive pity, that the seed of that message had fallen on stony ground, quick to spring up but quickly dying. Well, she knew now that in one instance at least it had rooted deeply.

'We're so very sorry.' Being sorry herself didn't help Phyllida's assumption of Miss Lubbock's sorrow. It was a paradox that had surprised her at the outset of her second career, but by now it was a familiar sensation: finding it harder to act out feelings she was experiencing herself than those that were no more than a part of her business skills – as it had been harder to convey to Jack, the terrible time she had been professionally forced to walk away from him, that she was sorry she had to go...

'Thank you,' Roma said. 'It's too, too dreadful. But we must all remember that Stan is safe; we mustn't mourn him.' Again, no overt evidence of irony, but Phyllida couldn't help suspecting it behind the calm, intelligent face. 'I mean, that's why we're here, isn't it?'

'Of course!' Marian managed a watery smile, looking round the room as if she had just had another revelation. 'Stan shouldn't have gone before his time, the Enabler forbids it and it was wrong. But he's safe, he's across the Bridge.'

'Across the Bridge,' Denis repeated, standing by the door with a hand raised, and, as if he had been their choirmaster, everyone but she and Sally, it seemed to Phyllida, took up the encouraging chant. Even Samantha Mason, she noted sadly, had mouthed the mantra, and her eyes now were sparkling with hope.

'There you are, Miss Lubbock!' Denis said, unbending sufficiently to offer her a brief smile and Sally a slightly longer one. 'Your presence here has helped us already.'

'Thank you, but I can't take the credit.' Miss Lubbock eased herself into the indicated corner of the sofa. 'It was Roma who set you back on the path.'

Roma flashed her a look in which surprise and appreciation were mingled. It was the first expression Phyllida had seen in her face beyond the very slight amusement that seemed to be her habitual look.

'It's pretty obvious,' Roma said. 'So no more gloom. If he'd broken his back, and lived on in this world...'

There was a shocked murmur, followed by a rustle of relief as people changed their positions to chime with their change of mood.

'Coffee for Miss Lubbock and Sally!' Denis said. 'Marian! It's her turn tonight,'

140

he explained hastily to Sally, who had not managed to keep a slight look of surprise out of her face at his peremptory tone.

Marian, though, had got immediately to her feet, with a smile. 'What would you both like. Tea? Coffee?'

Both again ordered coffee, and while they awaited it, the conversation, although subdued and intermittent, was cautiously cheerful, even optimistic. A little gentle fun was poked at Tom and Felicity, sitting with their arms round one another.

'The inseparables,' Roma explained to Sally and Miss Lubbock. 'When the time comes, they'll have both hands clasped.' It took a few moments for the comparative subtlety of Roma's comment to be taken in, but when it was it received looks of embarrassed approval. Phyllida, for a wild moment, wondered if Roma was the devil's advocate of The Bridge, there was such a contrast between the sophistication of her voice and what it was saying.

'Faiths unshaken' – Sally summed up what they had learned in Denis's flat as she shut Miss Lubbock's front door and snatched off her wig. 'Phew! You must feel awfully stuffy sometimes.'

'At the beginning. I lose it when I start performing. Like one does onstage.' Phyllida lifted off her own wig and shook out her short brown bob. 'But yes, it's always a good moment, shedding it all and coming back to oneself.'

So long as one was sure who that self was. As she and Sally flopped into the two scratchy purple armchairs, blowing out their cheeks and grinning at one another, Phyllida thanked Jack yet again for his everlasting gift of her own identity.

Nine

On the morning of The Bridge Open Day, Miss Lubbock telephoned Denis Young at a quarter past eight.

'It's extremely disappointing, Denis,' she told him, 'but I'm not very well – a recurrent problem that I won't go into, but when it strikes, I have to let it take its course. Fortunately the attacks don't last for long, and I'm assured that they're not life-threatening. But I was very much looking forward to today. It's wretched timing.'

'Miss Lubbock ... I'm frightfully sorry.' Hardly to Phyllida's surprise, he sounded distracted, his real reactions focused on the ground-breaking day to come. 'Is there anything...?'

'Oh, no.' Miss Lubbock dismissed the

reflex almost emphatically. 'That's very kind of you, but no one can do anything. It's just a matter of riding it out. I shall probably be fine by tomorrow, which makes it all the more annoying.'

'I'm frightfully sorry,' came again, followed by a brief pause. 'I hope Sally, though ... unless you need her with you...'

'Goodness, no. I only need a bed and some peace and quiet. Sally's looking forward to today as much as I was, but as I can't be with her, we were wondering ... Denis, Sally has a friend in town, staying at the Golden Lion. An American lady she met when she was over there not long ago. I've met her too, on several occasions, and she's very charming. Sally's been enthusing to her about The Bridge and we were wondering ... could Sally possibly bring Peggie Santorini with her in my place? I wouldn't suggest it if I didn't know that Sally has got her really interested in your movement.'

It seemed a long wait, and Phyllida had time to construct the wording in which Miss Lubbock would in an hour or so's time inform Denis of her unprecedentedly speedy recovery; but when he responded it was clear that he approved the idea of Sally's alternative companion, and was hesitating only before the thought of making a decision for which he had no authority.

'I think that should be fine, Miss Lub-

143

bock,' he brought out eventually; 'although we'll all miss you, of course. It *was* announced that Bridge members could invite sympathetic friends and relatives to the Open Day, and I take it that you and Sally will shortly be returning your membership application forms.'

So Denis Young was neither as straight, nor as naive, as to be above blackmail. Phyllida grinned at a yawning, tousled Sally as she responded.

'That's right, dear. Just let me get my head round this little setback, and we'll be returning both the forms.' Phyllida thought fondly of the ultimately unassailable portals of the Golden Lion.

'Great. Well ... I'd love to give Sally and her friend a lift, but you'll appreciate that today of all days ... duties...'

'Of course! Anyway, Sally loves driving.'

'That's all right, then? I've given you the route.'

'She's been studying it. What time should they arrive?'

'Any time from eleven onwards. The Enabler's opening his main entertaining rooms to his guests, plus the chapel and the grounds, and it'll be informal until one o'clock, when he'll appear before everyone for the first time, and address us.'

'In the chapel? I didn't think—'

'Oh, no. The Enabler would like to make

the chapel the heart of his message, but it's still Church of England and would have to be deconsecrated. Anyway, I gather his sister wouldn't go along with that.'

'She doesn't belong to The Bridge?'

'I'm afraid not. I haven't met her, but she's said to be quite anti, actually. Anyway, the Enabler's address will be the high point of the day, although afterwards there'll be a buffet and guests can wander about again until four. It's very generous.'

'It is indeed. Now, Denis, as you've just told me, you have duties, and you must go and start carrying them out. Thank you for letting Sally bring Peggie.'

'Gosh, I'm not *letting* ... I mean, I don't have any authority; I'm just saying that it seems to me that bringing her fits with what the Enabler has said about his guests.'

'Of course. That's what *I* meant. Now, off you go. And have a wonderful day. I look forward to hearing all about it.'

'Thanks, Miss Lubbock. So sorry ... Goodbye, now.'

'How will we get to the Golden Lion?' Sally asked, as Phyllida hung up. 'Or do I mean, who will get to the Golden Lion?'

'You mean both, I suppose. Well, I think blonde Sally will go down to her car, where she'll wait for a few moments until a rather botchily put together Miss Bowden joins her. Once I'm away from this front door it

145

won't matter who sees me, and anyway, Miss Bowden's chief strength is her unmemorability. You'll be ready for the country, but to avoid any avoidable meetings at the Golden Lion I think you'd better stay upstairs with me while I become Mrs Santorini. And yes, you can watch me if you must. And yes again, Santorini does sound a bit like an upmarket ice cream, but the lady insists it's her name. Now, let's have some very quick toast and tea.'

'Why are you abandoning Miss Lubbock?' Sally enquired, when they had finished their small, hurried breakfast and given in to the magnetic pull of the sitting-room window.

'I know Bridge reactions to her, and there won't be any fresh ones. Peggie Santorini will be a lot more in-your-face – in a totally charming way, of course. Miss Lubbock was self-effacing because I wanted to observe while being unobserved. Mrs Santorini, I hope, will attract more positive reactions, which should help us to learn more about the people who do the reacting; and they're bound to be a bit less inhibited in their conversation with each other in the presence of a younger woman who at least looks less straight-laced than Miss L. Another thing, Sally: I've found with my American ladies that they can be much more forward than a Brit without causing offence. I suppose that's why I use them pretty regularly; and

146

they're glamorous, and I enjoy them.'

'It's a sort of science, isn't it – your costume sleuthing?'

'Not consciously, but I suppose I've learned a few basic principles from it about human behaviour.'

'It's going to be a nice day.'

For a moment of silence they surveyed the vast scene, even the ugly grey foreground touched with a mixture of mist and sparkle that made Phyllida think of an old steel engraving of the early impact of the Industrial Revolution on a rural landscape. The distant prospect wasn't as rural as it looked, of course, but under another high, hazy sun, and in contrast with what lay between it and the building in which she and Sally stood, it was a promised land...

'To work!' Phyllida whirled away. 'I'm going to take on Miss Bowden in private, Sally – this morning I'll be cutting corners.'

But the woman who emerged from Miss Lubbock's bedroom twenty minutes later still elicited an admiring wolf whistle from Sally.

'That's the only one of *those* Miss Bowden will ever get – or will ever have had, I imagine, poor woman.' Phyllida spoke and smiled as herself, but when she turned round from the spotted overmantel mirror, her transformation was complete.

'Down you go, Sally!' Miss Bowden

ordered. 'I shan't be long after you. And if Denis Young sees you get into the lift, he won't be hovering outside *this* front door.'

'Your poor skin,' Sally said again as, less than ten minutes later, Miss Bowden climbed neatly into the passenger seat beside her. 'It's going to have to go through it all again in a few moments.'

'At least I've got a rest today from Miss Lubbock's mouth padding,' Phyllida said, as Sally roared into the main road. 'My most trying make-up to date was the Miss Pym I had to wear for such long stretches when I was your house guest.'

'Oh, Phyllida. I remember your sharp reaction when I suggested bringing Miss Pym breakfast in bed, it was so un-Miss-Pym-like. At the time I thought it was just old-fashioned modesty. I couldn't think it was because you didn't want to be seen without your teeth, because yours were so obviously your own and teeth are something you can't disguise, unless you put another set in front of them. Have you ever done that?'

'Not yet. Sally, this isn't Jehu's chariot, and we're all right for time.'

They parked behind the Golden Lion close to Phyllida's own car, which, following Sally's entrée into the investigation, there had been no need to expose to the higher risk level of the windswept parking ground

in the lee of the Heights. Phyllida had trans-
ferred her anxiety to Sally's car, but Peter's
undertaking that any loss or damage would
be made good by the Agency, coupled with
Sally's airy dismissal of Phyllida's concern,
had made it fairly easy to decide to remove
her car to comparative safety. There was
also, of course, the outside chance that
Denis Young, or another Bridge member,
just might be paranoid enough to seek a
number check on Miss Lubbock's car,
although both Phyllida and Peter had long
agreed that there were certain distant
prospects of discovery that they could not
allow themselves to be hobbled by...

'This is so much more exciting than Miss
Lubbock!' Sally breathed from another
corner chair, as Phyllida emerged from her
office bathroom in Mrs Santorini's coffee-
coloured, ecru-lace-trimmed satin under-
wear.

'Sure, honey.' They exchanged grins as
Phyllida slipped into an equally glossy
cream two-piece, and another one through
the looking glass when Phyllida had sat
down before it and was fastening gold
chains around her neck and a wrist. This
was followed by the descent of a shiningly
abundant dark-blonde wig and then – most
intriguingly of all to Sally – a gradual
change in the expression of the face in the
mirror: an imperceptible tautening of its

lines, a noticeable tilt of the head on what Sally suddenly realized was a long neck, and a rueful lopsidedness of the mouth in the smile that now met hers through the glass.

'Wow!' Sally whispered. 'You'll upstage the master!'

'No way; but I might get some attention. And when I speak, people may listen, and then try to please this attractive foreigner with their answers.'

'You're so ridiculously modest, I never thought I'd hear you call yourself attractive.'

Phyllida turned round from the glass, and Mrs Santorini's easy expression grew very slightly exasperated. 'You still haven't got the point, have you, honey? I'm not calling Phyllida Moon attractive, for God's sake; it's me I'm talking about, Peggie Santorini, who'd be crazy as well as blind if she didn't accept her looks.'

'It must be great to turn heads wherever you go,' Sally suggested wistfully.

'It's fun – in short doses.' It was Phyllida who spoke then, curt in contrast to Peggie Santorini, and doubly so because of being a bit ashamed of her enjoyment of her American woman's charisma. 'So let me look at *you* now, Sally ... I think the other night you had a bit more colour on the cheekbones. Go into the bathroom and see if I'm right. Otherwise even I wouldn't know you from a quick glance.'

'Mrs Santorini might invite her young friend to dinner in the hotel restaurant tonight,' Phyllida said, as countryside began to predominate over buildings and the traffic eased. 'If a Bridgeite spots them, which is pretty unlikely, they'll be behaving in character. It would be nice to include Jeremy in the role of blonde Sally's boyfriend, but we'd have to disguise him, and the day will be fraught enough – let's hope! – without a complication we don't need.'

'Away on business anyway,' Sally announced.

'Is he still happy – well, not unhappy – about what you're doing?'

'Yes. Truthfully. I know him well enough to be sure.'

'Good. But I'm sorry you can't tell him how long all this will be going on. We haven't done anything yet, Sally, beyond getting some information.'

'Isn't that a PI's brief? Getting information?'

'Yes. Of course. It's just that ... I think this particular client is hoping for more.'

On her second visit to Fifield Place Phyllida found the car park full, and another, bumpier area of shrubbery designated as the reserve. A youngish man, dour-faced, whom she didn't recognize, directed them into it, and the fact that his eyes flickered as Mrs Santorini alighted, and his Adam's apple did a bob, brought a discreet whoop of triumph from Sally.

'From now on, honey,' Peggie Santorini drawled as they strolled towards the house, 'we take each other – and whatever effects we create – for granted.'

'Of course. Sorry. Hi, there's old Denis! And the lovebirds!'

On the lower steps of the symmetrical stone flight leading up to the open front door from the left, Denis Young was standing tense and upright between Tom and Felicity, who were leaning back against the inner stone rail with their arms round one another, and two other young figures as obviously relaxed, side by side with their backs to the drive. If the DCS hadn't withheld from the media the discovery of a leaflet in Stan Dolby's pocket, Phyllida reflected, there would not have been this degree of relaxation.

'Roma and Colin,' Sally murmured, and Peggie Santorini turned to her with a challenging smile. 'Care to introduce me, honey?'

'Hi there, Denis!' If Sally was nervous, she wasn't showing it, although Phyllida noted that her circling glance passed quickly on from Roma's sleepily raking appraisal of both the newcomers, settling on Tom and Felicity whenever it moved from Phyllida. 'This is my friend Peggie Miss Lubbock was telling you about. Peggie, this is Denis. Felicity and Tom. Roma and Colin. No point in surnames en masse, one never remembers them.'

'Sally ... Peggie...' Denis smiled foolishly from one to the other.

'The English don't, but I've found that Americans are rather better,' Roma observed lazily, pulling herself forward from the support of the balustrade. 'How do you do, Peggie? Welcome to the biggest event The Bridge has ever staged.' Irony again, perhaps, and Phyllida saw Colin's lips twitch.

'I gather so. I feel very privileged to be here,' Mrs Santorini drawled. 'Although of course I'm sorry my gain should be your aunt's loss, honey.'

'She *is* very disappointed, but she's grateful for Peggie's invitation, Denis.' Sally looked round. 'No Marian? Charlie? Sam?'

'I've seen Charlie,' Denis said. 'And I saw Sam, but she disappeared before I had a chance to have a word with her.'

'I heard she's been called to the Presence,' Roma said. 'Sometimes the Enabler gives private audience to his followers,' she explained to Peggie and Sally.

'It's an enormous honour,' Denis contributed wistfully. 'It's happened to you, hasn't it, Roma? And I think you too, Colin? I'm still waiting,' he said with a thin smile, as they both nodded.

153

'I suspect the Enabler considers you to be strong enough in the faith, Denis, without a boost.' Roma's tone was less teasing than usual, and Denis's face lit up.

'You really think so?'

'I really do.'

'An English stately home!' Mrs Santorini enthused, surveying the surrounding scene. 'I've seen so many pictures of them, but although I've been to your country before, I've never gotten to see one.'

'This isn't exactly a stately home,' Denis said pedantically. 'I mean, you won't find it in any guidebook. It's a private house, but it *is* quite grand. The Enabler's offering us the freedom of the grounds today, and the two most important rooms inside the house. It's very generous.'

'Well, we are his flock, Denis,' Roma reminded him, then turned to Peggie. 'Have you been anywhere in the house or garden yet?'

'We've only just arrived,' Sally said, 'but we'd love to look around.'

Denis glanced at his watch, then uncertainly up at Phyllida and Sally, turning his gaze from one to the other as he spoke. *Spoilt for choice*, Phyllida thought, with an inward giggle: as a man of dreams rather than fulfilments, Peggie Santorini's age and sophistication would attract rather than deter him. 'Look,' he said. 'I can spare a few minutes. How about if I set you on your way inside, before it gets too crowded?'

'There are signposts, Denis,' Roma said, 'and plaques to be read. They should be able to manage. Anyway, Colin and I are about to go round inside; they can come with us if they feel they need company.' Roma's tone, though teasing, was gentle, and Denis's sigh and shake of the head were theatrical enough to make Phyllida decide that this sort of exchange had happened before and that these opposites were more at home with each other than she had supposed.

'All right,' he said. 'Mr Dixon wants to see me as soon as possible, so I ought to be on my way really. I'll see you both later,' he promised Phyllida and Sally as he descended the last three steps of the staircase.

'Dear old Denis,' Roma said, as his dogged stride took him quickly out of sight round the side of the house. 'You don't have to come with Colin and me, of course,' she said to Peggie and Sally; 'but I thought you might like to be delivered from his hovering presence, well intentioned as it would be.'

'I guess that was thoughtful,' Peggie said, 'although I haven't met Denis before.'

'He's all right,' Roma said, 'just a bit enthusiastic at times. What are you lovebirds doing?'

'We've been round the house when it was

open to the public,' Tom said, as he and Felicity reluctantly removed their eyes from each other. 'So we thought we'd have a stroll round the garden. The house is really worth a look,' he said to Phyllida and Sally. 'Some great furniture.'

'Good,' Sally said. 'We'll enjoy it; and we'd like to start off with you and Colin, Roma, even if we drift apart as we go along. All right, Peggie?'

'Sure, honey. Lead on, Colin!'

The imposing doors to drawing room and dining room were wide open, but the third, and identical, door leading off the hall was closed, and a small brass plaque in its centre announced 'Private'.

Peggie Santorini didn't notice this door until she had had her delighted fill of the open rooms and she and Sally were back in the hall, ending up only a few steps behind Roma and Colin, with whom they had kept pace round the rooms without carrying out identical tours.

' "Private",' Mrs Santorini read out. 'What room would that be, do you know, Roma? It looks just as important as the others.'

'That's the library, but the Enabler uses it as his study and sitting room. It isn't open to the public, but we'll be in there later when he speaks to us.'

'The family are very generous with what they let the public see,' Colin said. 'This is the only major room they keep private; and I believe that even that—'

He broke off as the door they were contemplating was pulled violently inwards and Samantha Mason came tumbling out, flushed and with eyes ablaze.

'Sam!' Sally put a hand out, but Samantha ignored it and ran across the hall, through the open front door, pausing against a pillar just outside with bent, heaving shoulders.

All eyes followed her, but Phyllida withdrew hers in time to see the door Sam had burst through pulled gently shut from the inside.

'Oh, dear,' Roma murmured. 'Oh, dear. "I have been half in love with easeful death." '

'What's that, honey?'

'Keats. "Ode to a Nightingale".'

'Ah. Excuse me a moment, will you?' Sam was still leaning against the pillar, but had pulled out a handkerchief and was blowing her nose. 'I guess we Americans can be a bit sentimental, but I don't like to see...'

With a pacifying smile round the group, fractionally quelling as it reached Sally, Mrs Santorini walked swiftly towards the outer door – not quite swiftly enough, though, to prevent Samantha suddenly bolting away from her prop and disappearing down one of the flights of steps.

Without looking back Phyllida followed, calling out to the girl as she neared the car parks.

'Hi, there! Honey! You all right?'

Samantha had at least halted, was looking back in what appeared to Phyllida's astonishment to be fear and loathing.

'Wait! Please.'

The urgency in Phyllida's voice had been out of character for Mrs Santorini, but it had brought the girl to a halt, even though she was tossing her long hair and kicking a pebble about, like a filly pawing the ground before taking off once more.

'What do you want?'

'Just to make sure you're all right, honey. Something's obviously upset you, and you shouldn't drive off feeling like that; it's not a good idea at all. How about if we just talk a few moments, you maybe get something off your chest? It's always good to—'

'There's nothing to talk about!' Sam suddenly spat, whirling round on Phyllida. 'Nothing at all. There never was, but I was such a fool...' Tears welled again, but she wiped them impatiently away with a bare hand. 'There's nothing there!' she shouted. 'Nothing but a dirty, filthy ... Oh, God.'

'Shall I sit in the car a moment with you, honey?'

'No, no, I'm all right. I'm going home!' For an instant the tragic face lightened. 'Thanks, though; you've been awfully kind.' Phyllida could see that Samantha had only just become properly aware of another presence. 'You don't know me and yet you've followed me ... I'm grateful, honestly I am.'

'That's all right, honey. So long as you promise me you really are going home.'

'I really am. Straight there. I promise.'

'All right, then. I'll see you off. Good luck, honey.'

'Good luck ... Sorry, I don't know your name. Mine's Samantha.'

'And mine's Peggie. Off you go, now.'

The second Samantha Mason's small car had disappeared round the first curve of the drive, Phyllida was on her mobile to Peter.

Ten

'Did you discover what *that* was all about?' Roma inquired, as Peggie Santorini rejoined the small group that was now standing at the foot of one of the flights of stone steps. Phyllida had walked back slowly, to be sure of regaining her breath in time to present Mrs Santorini's usual serene demeanour.

'I'm afraid not, honey. But I did get a promise out of her that I think she'll keep – to go straight home. Have any of you any idea of what can have happened?'

Sally shrugged and, after a glance at Roma, Colin spoke, with a nonchalance that Phyllida suspected of being contrived, while warning herself against believing she was seeing something simply because she wanted to see it.

'The Enabler's presence can be quite painfully powerful. I suppose it must just have been too much for her.'

'Ah. Yes, of course.' *Filthy*. A word to be reserved for Miss Moon's report on the day, although Phyllida suspected she would share it later with Sally.

'Would you like to see round the garden?' Roma turned from Peggie to Sally, then stiffened slightly. 'Ah ... Charlie.'

'Cheers.' Puffing slightly, Charlie drew up beside them. 'Just been round the garden. Not all of it as sleek as the part you can see. Lots of slopes and wild bits. Worth a look.'

Charlie had been glaring suspiciously at Mrs Santorini as she spoke and, relishing the challenge, Phyllida had met her stare with a slight rueful smile, which to her triumph elicited a brief baring of teeth in response as Charlie fell silent.

'May I introduce my friend Peggie Santorini?' Sally said. 'She's from America, and she's very interested in The Bridge.'

'Humph.' Phyllida thought it was the first time she had heard someone actually say that. 'Lots of funny ideas over there. Glad

160

you've found *us*. You're pretty damned lucky to have coincided with today.'

'I believe so,' Peggie responded humbly. 'I guess I'm blest.'

'Well, if you know that...' Charlie further relented. 'See you later, I expect,' and she went marching off.

'Charlie Parkinson,' Colin explained. 'Butch, I would say, but there's no partner in evidence. Very keen Bridgeite.'

'Her style of speech tends to be catching,' Roma said, with a sideways smile at Colin. 'The garden, then? Hello, Marian. We're just going round the garden, if you'd fancy joining us. This is Mrs Santorini, a friend of Sally's.'

'Thanks, but I think I'll ... just contemplate on one of those seats until it's time.' Trying to decide what was different about the mousey girl she had twice encountered in Denis Young's flat, Phyllida decided it was a species of irradiation from within giving her an incorporeal look that had not been in evidence when she and Phyllida had met before, and had to subdue a sudden shiver of reminiscent horror at the evidence through history of the power of the demagogue.

But Colin had seen it. 'Are you cold, Peggie?'

'No. Just the proverbial goose on my grave, I guess'; but she was in the field, and this time managed to suppress another shiver at the thought of the ever-present possibility that what Peggie Santorini had just said might turn out to be more than a trite little joke. 'Gee, this is a pretty fine place!'

Close to the house, the garden was eighteenth-century swathes of lawn right to the windows, but another, and longer, flight of balustraded stone steps below the grassed slope on the south side led down to a formal layout of flower beds bordered by an intricate pattern of low box hedges, a stone fountain playing in their midst. Below that again, more steps took them to the wooded, wilder area approved by Charlie, where orange and lemon-coloured azaleas glowed among the small green fists of new leaves on the tall trees that allowed only thin shafts of sunlight to penetrate. On their way back they paused at the top of the higher flight of steps and looked out over the sunken tree-tops to a pattern of small hedged fields gently undulating into the haze of the horizon.

'It's beautiful!' Sally exclaimed, 'and not a high-rise or even a housing estate in sight!'

'It's countryside, not green belt,' Roma said. 'So it has to be under threat. Everything naturally beautiful in today's world makes me feel sad, because I fear for it.'

'That's so right, honey,' Mrs Santorini

said, as Phyllida decided that she liked this unreadable woman.

'The chapel now, I think,' Colin said, 'and its fearsome guardian.'

'That'll be the Enabler's sister, I suppose?' Sally said, as they turned reluctantly from the panorama and started to climb the grassy slope back to the house. 'Denis was telling us ... Miss Lubbock and me' – Sally offered a quick apologetic glance at Miss Lubbock's successor – 'that she doesn't go along with The Bridge and won't consider letting it have the chapel.'

'That's true.' Roma turned for a last look across the garden. 'But even if she did go along with us, I doubt the Church Commissioners, or whoever it is has the say-so, would allow such a precedent. So jolly old C of E the place remains.'

'Does The Bridge clash with the established religions, then?' Mrs Santorini enquired.

'Oh, yes,' Colin answered promptly, as they rounded the house on the chapel side. 'Bridgeites are agnostics in every way save for their knowledge of the friends waiting to help them when the time comes for them to cross to the next world. For us, parts of any of the established religions may be true, just as they may not. We believe that we don't, and can't, know.'

'I guess that's a refreshingly simple philosophy,' Peggie drawled. 'I like it more and more. I've never been happy with the gods of human invention.' Phyllida was again uneasily aware of the paradox that when her own basic views coincided with the basic views of her characters she felt her thespian skills to be in sudden jeopardy. 'People have done terrible things through history to the people who don't see life and death their way.'

'You'll like it more still – you may love it,' Roma said – 'when you've heard the Enabler. Here we go.'

For a moment the dim interior seemed to be deserted, but within seconds Hermione Henderson was striding towards them, a taller, slimmer and slightly more feminine version of Charlie, with the same suspicious gaze.

'Ah! Some more of Charles's party. Hope you won't find a fine Anglican interior too absurd!'

'I guess we won't find it absurd at all!' Mrs Santorini quickly responded.

'It's part of our history, I'm afraid,' Roma said, turning to grimace at Colin as his elbow dug into her side.

'I think it's beautiful!' Sally exclaimed. 'Can you tell us about it?'

'Well ... yes, of course I can ... if you really want to know.'

'We really do,' Peggie Santorini assured her. 'I personally would be very disappointed to leave without the benefit of your knowledge.'

'Beautifully put,' Roma whispered, as Miss Henderson turned away on a sharp 'Follow me, then!'

Phyllida had heard the commentary before, but had found it interesting enough to enjoy the repetition and to feel as they blinked their way back into the sunshine that the twenty minutes had passed swiftly, despite Roma's ostentatious yawns. Sally, of course, was all enthusiasm, although she made it plain to her companions that what interested her was the aesthetics and the history, rather than the fact of being in a place of Christian worship.

'Yes, well,' Roma said, when Sally had completed her eulogy, 'the real experience is yet to come.' She glanced at her watch. 'And pretty soon. So let's go take our places.'

'So we'll see the library!' Sally exclaimed excitedly, as they climbed the nearer set of steps to the front door.

'We will – if not its inner sanctum. There's little limit to our leader's generosity.'

'You've been in the library before? Roma? Colin?'

'In our time,' Roma said, after another little smile at Colin.

'The inner sanctum,' Mrs Santorini drawled. 'What is that?'

'An inside room off the main library, not

accessible from anywhere else. No one ever gets inside there, except, I suppose, the family, and Mr Dixon.' This time Roma's smile was for herself. Had the context been different, Phyllida would have described it as reminiscent. 'It's where the Enabler contemplates, meditates, gathers strength.'

The door marked 'Private' was open when they entered the hall, and Mr Dixon was standing beside it, wearing the neat grey suit he had worn in Barton Street or its twin, and the same gravity of expression; but as Roma and her party came up to him, he offered a thin smile.

'Welcome, welcome,' he said. 'Please enter and find yourself seats.'

Phyllida's first reaction was that this room, although currently defaced by several rows of small camp chairs filling its central space, was the most elegant of the three important downstairs chambers: glass-fronted bookshelves in glowing light oak covered two of the walls and stood to each side of a fire surround that could only be described as important, its black-and-grey marble adorned with classical scenes in high relief. The fourth wall had two long small paned windows whose elegance, Phyllida decided, had to reflect their adherence to the golden section. Between them stood a gracefully substantial table-desk, topped with an elaborate silver inkwell and a small tidy heap of papers.

A studied study, Phyllida reacted as she looked around; but all in the best of historical taste, and the deep leather armchairs to each side of the fireplace looked comfortable and sufficiently shabby.

The increasing human content of the room, although it appeared – apart from Charlie – noticeably awed (Marian, entering alone just behind them, had tears on her cheeks), looked not unlike a theatre or concert audience and gave off none of the reluctance, or the furtive air, that had characterized the majority of those taking their seats in the De Luxe cinema – which was why, of course, no more than four rows of a dozen seats had been provided. This was the paid-up membership, and those hovering on the edge of it – a tiny number of people in a world teeming with spiritual movements, but rapt enough not to be discouraged by the knowledge Phyllida would have been unable to suppress: that they were so very few to have been entrusted with the truth.

Watching them quietly taking their places, Phyllida found it hard to imagine that what had so recently upset Samantha Mason had taken place in this tranquil chamber, and she looked wistfully towards the narrow door into the inner sanctum which was the only break in the wall of bookshelves facing the fireplace.

'Here, I think,' Roma said, the natural leader, spearheading their weave a little way into the second row on the window side. The seats had been placed to face a lectern with a few sheets of paper on it set in the angle between the windows and that inner door. There was a small low table under the nearer window, on which stood a carafe of water and a glass within reach of a speaker's hand, and a chair with a green leather seat to the other side of the inner door. Following the entry of the last of the Bridgeites came the small figure of Mrs Henderson, whom Mr Dixon welcomed with a bow. Phyllida had assumed that he would lead her to the leather seat, but their unhesitant walk to the comparatively distant small armchair beside the long wall of bookcases facing the windows was obviously by prior agreement.

'The lady's too self-effacing for Speakers' Corner,' Roma whispered to Peggie Santorini, and this latest irony made Phyllida finally decide that Roma's mickey-taking attitude to the creed she ostensibly followed had to be akin to the jokes she had heard Catholics tell against themselves because they were so secure and comfortable in their faith. If she was wrong, well ... Samantha Mason had fled The Bridge and would surely not return. Unless Maurice Kendrick wanted more information about the creed and its adherents in his professional capacity, by the time she and Sally drove away, her assignment would be over.

'Friends' – it was Mr Dixon who had claimed the green leather chair, and was standing in front of it. Phyllida found it hard to imagine the imminent eclipse of his strong, deep voice by one even more powerful. 'Welcome to this unique and historic occasion.' How much did he believe of what he was saying? There was no trace of irony in *his* voice, but Phyllida didn't find it hard to imagine a cynicism behind those calm eyes, as grey as his suit, which she suspected could be viewing The Bridge as a commercial venture with possibilities of lucrative expansion.

'The Enabler has done us the honour of inviting us into his home, and consenting to address us here. When he has spoken, he will invite you all into his dining room, which is at this moment being set with a repast of which you are all invited to partake.' No notes, but it sounded as if he was reading – and effectively, to have sidestepped bathos and elevated a buffet lunch to the status of a Last Supper. 'You are also welcome to continue your enjoyment of the gardens until four o'clock, when house and grounds will be closed. There is no charge, friends, for today's privileges, but the copper bowl on the hall table may be used by those who wish to express their gratitude to the Enabler for his generosity with a contribution to Bridge funds. And now, friends, what we have all been waiting for, the climax of this unique day.'

Mr Dixon turned slowly to face the small door beside him, raised his hand, and gave two soft taps upon it. Phyllida heard catches of breath from all around her as Mr Dixon withdrew his hand and they waited for what she counted as ten seconds before the door slowly opened and the Enabler stood before them. Seen close to, and in a smaller space than the stage and auditorium of the De Luxe cinema, the impact of his height, raised hands and composite look of Victorian renditions of Old Testament prophets was immensely powerful, and Phyllida heard the corporate caught breath release itself in long exhalations.

'My dear, dear people...' If the lectern hadn't stood between the speaker and his audience Phyllida imagined those in the front row physically cowering before the impact of the figure plus the voice, which seemed to define the shape of the room, resonating into its every angle. 'I welcome you to my home with the same love, and the same joy, with which I welcome you to the certainty of your survival. This house has stood strong and sound for three hundred years; but you, my friends, will stand strong and sound for ever...'

Phyllida was aware of a sudden slight roughness entering the ringing tones in the moment the Enabler stretched out his hand towards the carafe of water on the table beside him. She registered with amusement the continuing awed silence in which his audience watched him take the glass off the neck of the carafe, pick up the carafe with his other hand, pour some water, take a deep swallow of the liquid, and set the glass back on the table.

'My dear, dear friends,' the Enabler repeated, sniffing slightly, 'I cannot tell you too often of that enormous joy—'

The voice cut off abruptly as the outstretched hands flew upwards, the fingers stretching into rigidity as the body arched, then the arms falling as the whole man fell, sending the lectern toppling at the feet of the people in the front row, Charles Henderson sprawled face down across its pedestal, the crack of jawbone on wood eliciting a collective wince that was a separate reflex from the shock of witnessing the fall of an idol.

Phyllida turned her head farther to the left and saw the Enabler's wife start up from her seat, stand still for a moment with hands clenched at her sides and then, as the shock in her face faded to a total lack of

171

expression, come running forward to push her way through the gathering group and drop to her knees beside the fallen giant, putting her hand in a clearly professional gesture around one of the outstretched wrists.

'She was a nurse,' Roma breathed.

'He's dead.' Phoebe Henderson looked up at the clustering faces. 'Charles is dead.' She made an actor's gesture of sniffing the snarling lips. 'Because he's just drunk cyanide. Ring the police, Mr Dixon.' The voice was still soft, but no longer sweet 'Make sure nobody touches the glass or the carafe. In fact' – her smallness and lightness enabled her to rise gracefully to her feet – 'I'll take them into the sanctum and lock them up...'

'I don't think so, Phoebe.' With a gentle but firm gesture The Bridge's business manager stayed the hand stretching out for the glass and the carafe. 'I don't think they should be moved by anyone except the police. Fingerprints and the possibility of tampering unless they remain in public view – I'm sorry, but that has to apply to everyone.'

'Of course.' To Phyllida's surprise, Phoebe Henderson dropped her hand, and let Mr Dixon guide her to one of the vacated seats in the front row.

'Please move back,' he ordered, as he straightened up. 'We must not disturb the

172

scene of the crime.' Mr Dixon paused, looking broodingly at his hastily retreating audience. 'If that is what it is. We have to consider the possibility that our leader chose to leave us.'

'Never!' Mrs Henderson was on her feet again, the hitherto lifeless eyes blazing.

'He always told us how wrong it would be to anticipate our crossing,' some female voice shouted.

'Oh, yes.' There was an expression now on Phoebe Henderson's face as she raked the huddle of people with her large pale-blue eyes. Contempt, Phyllida read with surprise. But for whom? 'He told us that. And he loved life far too well to cut his own short.'

'Phoebe...' Mr Dixon was taking her arm again, suggesting she sit down. 'I'll ring the police. And an ambulance. Although I'm afraid...'

'Yes. I told you. He's dead. You don't drink water laced with cyanide and stay alive.'

'No.' Mr Dixon crossed the room to the fireplace, pulled on a silken cord, then walked to the door, opening it and standing in the gap for the few moments it took for a young woman to appear.

'Ask Miss Henderson to come to the library,' he said. 'Tell her it's urgent. And bring a jug of water and a glass. Quickly.'

'Yes, Mr Dixon.' But Phyllida saw the girl make an attempt to look past him before

173

flouncing off with a toss of the head as he manoeuvred his body to frustrate her and closed the door on her curiosity.

The words 'water' and 'glass' brought a collective hiss, to which Mr Dixon did not react. He stood by the door, motionless and with his head bowed, until his order was delivered, then crossed to the desk via the space at the back of the chairs, the tray in his hands bearing a carafe and a glass identical with those on the small table. The audience hissed again as they saw it.

'Please sit down,' Mr Dixon commanded, in rich diapason, and bit by bit he was obeyed. He set the tray down on the desk between the windows, poured water into the glass and took it over to Mrs Henderson. On the desk an old telephone stood like a black daffodil, its receiver hanging from a hook at the top of its graceful stem; but Mr Dixon ignored it, and murmured into a mobile. When he had returned it to his pocket, he stayed beside the desk to address them.

'We must, I am afraid, remain in this room until the police arrive. If ... ah ... anyone has need of bathroom facilities, I will call a member of staff to accompany them. Paramedics are on their way, but if they arrive before the police, they can do no more than confirm that our leader is dead.' An anguished female moan from somewhere behind Phyllida. 'They must leave him where he is until the police and their forensic colleagues have examined the scene of his death.'

'Of his murder,' Phoebe Henderson amended. Phyllida had watched her sip from the glass of water, and she was now sitting very still and upright, her unblinking forward gaze focused high above her husband's body...

'We don't know—' Mr Dixon began, and was interrupted by a fortissimo shout of 'Oh yes we do!' from Charlie.

'It has to be a crime!' Charlie bawled on. 'The Enabler would never end his life before its allotted time. *That* would be the crime, the crime against life that he, of all of us, would never commit!'

More comments followed, turning the gathering into a nightmare version of the Quaker funeral Phyllida had once attended, where friends and relatives of the deceased – decently coffined – had risen spontaneously to reminisce about his virtues. Under cover of the hubbub Mrs Santorini took out her own mobile phone and punched a number.

'Peter? Peggie Santorini here. Miss Lubbock wasn't well this morning, so Sally invited me in her place. Look, I'm afraid I'm not going to be able to make our meeting. Our host has just met with a fatal accident

175

and we're all confined in the library until the police arrive ... Yes, I know.' Phyllida's voice dropped to a whisper. 'All very dated but at least there isn't a butler. Sorry, it's not funny, it's awful, and I've gone out of character. One thing: perhaps it would be a good move to let Kendrick know why I'm delayed. And you can reassure him that his niece left Fifield Place over an hour ago.'

'It's all right,' Mrs Santorini drawled, smiling at Mr Dixon as his roving glance lighted on the phone in her hand. 'Cross my heart I wasn't alerting the press. I was just explaining to a friend I was meeting later that I don't expect to be able to make it. Sorry.'

'What's done is done. But please' – the rich voice rose again to full power – 'please all refrain from making calls before the police arrive. They'll be here very soon, and I don't think any of you will have appointments elsewhere within the next two or three hours. Now, please remain in your seats and try to wait quietly. Meditation may be in order.'

Now they obeyed him, on a collective murmur of approval. Only Denis Young continued to pace up and down beside the windows as if he had been programmed, and it took Mr Dixon's firmly guiding presence to steer him to his seat on the end of the front row, where he sank down with his

176

head in his hands, matching the stance of Marian beside him, if not her heaving shoulders.

This was the end of the blurted public comments, making it possible for Roma to murmur into Mrs Santorini's ear, 'I wouldn't put it past the old wizard to finish himself off in public, whatever he's been preaching. But he wouldn't do it when he'd hardly begun; he'd do it as the grand concluding gesture – which makes me pretty sure that our Enabler's been murdered.'

As she said the final word, her voice faltered and, turning to look at her, Phyllida was as surprised as she was shocked to witness what she could only define as a breaking up of Roma's calm face into an anguish of grief. Her serenity was restored as quickly as it had been lost, but this time Phyllida had no doubts about what she had witnessed.

Eleven

'Mum!'

'Sam! I thought it was your big day. Whatever are you doing at home?'

'I thought *you* were working...'

'Sorry to disappoint you, darling. Maureen wants tomorrow free, so she's swapped with me. I wasn't expecting to see you, but if you've brought some of your friends – sorry, colleagues – home, that's fine. I'll move into the small sitting room and you can take over in here ... Sam! Whatever is it?'

'Oh ... *Mum!*'

With a wail Samantha had hurled herself across the room and on to her knees in front of her astonished mother, who aborted her act of rising and sat back on the sofa so that Samantha could bury her head in her lap.

'Darling Sam, what is it?' Apprehension and concern were spreading through Mary in physical waves, but they couldn't subdue the delight of her daughter's tumbled hair spilling across her knees, the agitated burrowing movements Sam was making against her, and the girl's tolerance of her mother's hand stroking the remembered silky feel towards which it had yearned now for so many weeks.

'Oh, Mum ... Mum...' Sam didn't raise her head to speak, and Mary bent down to catch the sob-punctuated mumble. 'I've been such a *pig*. I've been so absolutely *horrible*. I've made you so unhappy. I knew I was doing it: part of me wanted to, part of me was *glad* when I'd pushed you away and I could see I'd hurt you; the other part of me wanted to stop, to say sorry, say I loved you, but the horrid part wouldn't let me...'

'I know, I know. It was losing Daddy—'

'This *Bridge* thing, it was because of Daddy ... I was missing him so much I couldn't help hoping ... but it was so *unfair*. It's been like I was blaming you because he wasn't here any more. And feeling there couldn't be any of you left over for me because you missed him so much.'

'But darling, I wanted to share ... I tried–'

'I know. I *know*. And I just went on making it all worse for you. You must have felt you'd lost us both.'

'I did. But now that you've seen it ... it's all wiped out, darling, all gone. And I never gave up believing I'd get you back.' She'd been on the edge of it, though.

'Oh, Mum!'

'Talking of getting back, Sam – what's happened to your special day? It's only half

179

past twelve.'

'Special day!' Now Sam jerked up, staring angrily into her mother's eyes. 'A dirty old man talking nonsense to a bunch of idiots!'

'Dirty old man? Not your – what is it – your Enabler?'

'*Yes!* Oh, Mum, I was summoned to the Presence, as they call it, and I thought wow! talk about privilege ... and when I went in – into an inner room where there was a *bed* – well, a couch – there was this old man who mumbled a few words about our eternal future and how we were all caught up in love or some other rubbish and then ... then ... was saying that love grew by expression, and then ... Ugh! I can hardly bear to say it. It was like he wanted a sacrificial virgin to give him oomph for his big performance.'

'Sam! He didn't...'

'No!'

But had anyone else? Mary hoped wistfully that Sam's choice of the word 'virgin' was to be taken literally as well as metaphorically, but a modern mother couldn't ask...

'Not for want of trying, though. He was suddenly all over me, one hand between my legs – thank God for jeans – and one pulling at a nipple and his great body pushing me towards this couch. I don't know how I did it – desperation, I guess – but I managed to knee him where it hurt, and while he was

180

doubling up I fled into the library that this room was off, and out into the main hall. I was terribly afraid at least one of the doors would be locked, but he must have been so confident. God, Mum, I feel sick every time I think of it. And I've started to think – those girls I've met, has he tried ... has he *actually made it* with some or all of them?'

'If he's tried, perhaps he has, or they'd have run off like you did. He was taking a terrible risk. And your ... your beliefs must have taken a terrible knock. I'm so sorry, darling.'

'My beliefs!' Sniffing, Sam scrambled up on to the sofa and nestled close to her mother. 'My beliefs vanished into the lust in that old goat's face. And all they were really was hoping to get in touch with Daddy, though I almost made myself believe in the whole crappy business. God, it was crazy! I still buy the idea of not subscribing to the orthodox religions, but I bought that before I met The Bridge. The Bridge! What a load of old rubbish! And that disgusting old man...' Samantha shuddered, then sprang to her feet. 'I'm going upstairs for a shower. It won't wash the disgust away, but it'll have to make my body feel cleaner.'

'Did anyone see you run off, Sam?'

'I suppose so; there were people milling about outside the sacred door ... Well, yes, 'cos an American woman followed me. I stopped just outside the front door to sort of pull myself together before going for the car; I knew he wouldn't dare follow me. And it was when I'd gone down the steps to the drive and was going pretty quickly towards the car park that I heard this woman calling. I can't remember just what I said. It wasn't much, but it must have been enough for her to make me promise to go straight home. She was sort of mature glamorous, and I thought it was nice of her to bother to come after me.'

'Yes – to take the trouble.' Like someone on a job for her brother would. 'Was she ... was she with anyone you know?'

'I think she'd come with Sally, though I'm not sure; I'd never seen her before. But I can't imagine her being taken in by all that rubbish. Oh, Mum, all those nights in the rain, grinning and dishing out crap ... I can't bear to think about it!'

'Then try not to. Go and get your shower, and when you come down, there'll be sherry and scrambled egg.'

Sam's new self-doubt appeared to preclude the audible slamming of upstairs doors, but after listening to the silence for a long five minutes Mary rang the police. Told that her brother was out of the office, she left a message to say she'd called and would call again, but that he was not to call her.

So her initial reaction was annoyance,

swamped by fear for her reconciliation with her daughter, when the telephone rang during their trolley lunch and she heard his sombre tones the other end of the line.

'Mary. Maurice here.'

'I said ... Look, I'm afraid it's ... inconvenient ... at the moment. I'll call you later.'

'I'm not ringing you back. I have some information. I'm at Fifield Place. Charles Henderson's dead, probably murdered, and there's no sign of Samantha.'

Not for the first time, Mary Mason marvelled that her brother had risen so high in his career, given the minimal interpersonal skills he tended to exhibit in his dealings with her. It had to be, she supposed, that when he was dealing outside his family, he forced himself to work on it.

'That's all right, Maurice. She's here – eating lunch with me at this very moment. Very much an ex-Bridgeite. She arrived home about half an hour ago.'

'And an hour on the road ... Thank God. She's clear, Mary.'

'Could you have doubted it?'

'Circumstance ... Why is she home?'

'Because the man you've just said is dead tried to rape her.' Sam's fork clattered to her plate as she turned towards her mother, a hand at her heart. 'Look, Maurice, she's just heard me say that, so I must fill her in on the other half of this conversation. And a bit

183

more, if only to be fair. How did he die?'

'Poison. Probably cyanide. In a glass of water. Could just have been self-inflicted, but I'm inclined not to think so – all the more so in the light of what you've just told me about him vis-à-vis Sam ... Off you go, and fill her in. I'll be with you when I can get away from here. We've a houseful of hysterics to try to get talking sense.'

He hadn't been exaggerating, Kendrick told himself with a sigh as he pocketed his mobile and emerged reluctantly from the downstairs loo where he had taken temporary refuge. They had to be unbalanced for a start, to be where they were, and he could hear voices raised in protesting shock and disbelief when he was still some way from where they were confined; but the fact that Sam was out of it both physically and mentally was an antidote to the weariness that overcame him at the mere thought of the difficult interviews to come, even though she was the reason he was going to have to suggest – if not today – that there might have been an extra dimension to the relationship of their leader with his female adherents. Sam's release, in fact, was his imprisonment in what could become a public scandal, Kendrick mentally summarized as he knocked for admission to the library where it all awaited him. He felt confident, though, that the glow of Sam's deliverance would make him personally robust enough to withstand a media assault.

DS Fred Wetherhead was just inside the door as the uniform let him in, his craggy face as reassuring as ever. 'There's an inner room, sir. Only access from this one. Ideal set-up for interviews. Forensics are here, as you can see. I've called for screens.'

'Which should have been brought as a priority, for God's sake.' Kendrick looked from the purposeful white-coated huddle to the aimless group at the farther end of the room – just about equally divided between those who were doing their best to see what the team was up to and those who had turned their backs – then whirled round at the man on the door. 'Get those screens here, and in place,' he roared. *'Now!'*

'Yes; with what's going on open to view, it's a wonder we've been able to turn the fellow's audience into sheep' – DS Wether-head shot a troubled glance from one end of the room to the other – 'and herd them to the back without any trouble. Except for the sister, that is. She's been creating.'

'Lead me to her, Fred, if that's the case. I'll have what I hope will be a calming word before I speak to the team.'

A lead was scarcely necessary, although Kendrick let his DS precede him in the direction of the tall, strong looking woman whose body language as she shouted at the

185

impassive uniform standing beside her told Kendrick unambiguously of her sense of outrage and lese-majesty.

As Wetherhead and Kendrick approached, she swung round on them angrily, and the momentary reflex recoil – immediately overcome – with which she took in Kendrick made him yet again thankful for the imposing height that had her tilting her head back as she glared up at him.

'And you are?'

'Detective Chief Superintendent Maurice Kendrick. This is my sergeant, DS Wetherhead. You, I believe, are Miss Hermione Henderson.' An impatient nod. 'I'm very sorry, Miss Henderson, that this dreadful thing has happened to your brother.'

'I should think so! But I knew no good would come of this silly fad of his. The Bridge! He wanted it to take the chapel over – can you believe it? The chapel to a household of Christian people for three centuries! And all these crazy hangers-on drifting about. The man had gone out of his mind!' Making no concession to the defamatory nature of her comments, Miss Henderson voiced them as loudly as she had been voicing her general complaints, and Kendrick was aware of a change in the tone of some of the protests rumbling off the beleaguered Bridgeites, their confusion and dismay augmented by pockets of anger triggered by

Miss Henderson's diatribe, and reflected in the disarray of the canvas chairs on which some of them were sitting, no longer in neat rows but higgledy-piggledy now about the far end of the room from the prone figure at the heart of the white-coated, white-gloved tableau of figures fitfully spotlit by camera flashes. Kendrick could feel his own anger rising at the continuing nakedness of the scene, and it was a relief to his blood pressure as well as to his professionalism as the door opened and a couple of uniforms entered with a couple of large drawing-room screens incongruously decorated with scraps predominantly comprising rows of small Victorian girls interspersed with rows of dogs wearing coloured ribbons; but they were adequate for their exceptional purpose, and within seconds had hidden both the corpse and its attendants.

'So if you think your brother was mad, Miss Henderson,' Kendrick said, giving her his full attention, 'perhaps you also think that he took his own life?'

'I didn't say that! Madmen can be murdered just as well as the sane. There've been times when I could cheerfully have murdered him myself, and I can't believe there aren't others...' Following Miss Henderson's darting glance, Kendrick thought it had passed over both the small, fair woman in the depths of one of the large armchairs and a very neat man in a grey suit – the only two people, perhaps, who waited motionless and without facial expression.

'Indeed,' Kendrick responded, mildly. 'Now, though, if you will be good enough to be patient for a few moments, we'll take your statement first, as soon as I've had a word with my forensic team. In the meantime this officer will take names and addresses.'

As Miss Henderson flounced reluctantly into the unoccupied large armchair, shaking off the attempted guiding hand of the uniform as if it was a fly, Kendrick turned to survey the whole scattered group, raising his voice. 'If I may have your attention for a moment ... A cold meal has been laid out for you in the dining room, and we're arranging for the food and jugs of water to be brought to you in here. Please eat and drink while your particulars are being taken. I presume that's Dixon,' Kendrick continued sotto voce to his DS, giving a slight nod in the direction of the man in the grey suit. 'And the wife?' As he studied the woman deep in the other armchair, he saw that she was not as still as he had first thought: the hands in her lap were twitching and trembling.

'Right on both counts, sir. I think we could find Dixon a good witness.'

'Let's hope you're right.' Kendrick moved towards them. 'Mrs Henderson, I'm so very

188

sorry. Mr Dixon, you've clearly been a helpful influence here, and we appreciate it.' No reaction from either, beyond a flicker of eyelids. 'As soon as I've spoken with my forensic team, we'll start the interviews and taking of statements in the inner room. I think you'll both agree it will be advisable to begin with Miss Henderson, but as soon as we have her statement we'll talk to you both and then you can at least move to another part of the house.'

'Thank you' – the rich voice of the business manager. Mrs Henderson merely nodded without looking up, and before crossing the room Kendrick turned his attention back to the Enabler's erstwhile audience, feeling free at last to do what it had been his instinct to do the moment he had entered the room: to pinpoint Miss Lubbock.

'Has anyone been allowed to leave, sergeant?' Kendrick heard the sharpness in his voice as he turned to his DS.

'No one, sir.' It took only a few seconds for Fred Wetherhead's surprise to turn to understanding. 'You don't see her, sir?' he murmured.

'No. She isn't here.' It was academic now, of course: Sam was free of both brainwashing and murder inquiry; but he had commissioned a presence at this ridiculous gathering from the Peter Piper Agency and there should be one. 'Ah...'

'Yes, I was wondering, sir.' DS Wetherhead had been following Kendrick's gaze as it reached Mrs Santorini.

'Wonder no longer.' The handsome woman who was sitting on her canvas chair as if it was a small throne caught and held his eyes, nodded slightly and allowed her wry smile briefly to widen. As always, it annoyed Kendrick that he found Phyllida Moon's American women so attractive.

'But how can we...'

'She'll see to it.'

A moment or two after Kendrick and Wetherhead had emerged from behind the boards, gone into the inner room and closed the door behind them, Mrs Santorini had a word with her friend Sally, got to her feet, sauntered over to the hovering uniform, and asked him if he would accompany her to the little girls' room.

'The...? Oh, yes, of course, madam. My colleague at the door will escort you. I'll take you to him.'

Thankful for the shibboleth that keeps males out of female – even if only temporarily female – lavatories on every occasion short of apocalypse, Phyllida left her escort at the indicated door with a smile, and locked it behind her. Sitting down on the closed seat, she took out her mobile and dialled Kendrick's.

'Yes?'

190

'Phyllida here.'

'I thought so.'

'I'm sorry you weren't prepared for Mrs Santorini. I asked Peter to call you.'

'My mobile's been off. But I've spoken to my sister. Sam's safe home.'

'She promised. Mrs S is staying at the Golden Lion. I didn't know until this morning that Miss Lubbock would be out of action with a recurring health problem. Fortunately Sally was able to ask her friend Peggie to take her place, vouching for her enthusiasm. Maurice ... hold back on a woman called Roma Westlake. There was something in her reaction to the death ... and she made one comment that struck home. She said that if Henderson had planned to take his own life he'd have done it at the climax of his oration – the ultimate grand gesture. He wouldn't have done it before he'd even got properly started. It might be helpful if Peggie had a word with her first.'

'And if we leave Mrs Santorini till the last, or near the last, then maybe she can have a word with other witnesses as well.' The deep voice hesitated. 'I know Sam's safe, and what I came to the Agency for has been achieved, but we've worked together before when a misdemeanour's turned into a crime. Will you carry on in the usual way?'

'Of course. Mrs Santorini will have a word

191

with other witnesses.'

'Thank you. Anything else for now?'

'Mrs Henderson refused publicly to believe her husband could have committed suicide. He loved life too much to cut it short was the gist of her argument. No doubt she'll repeat herself to you.'

'If not, I can do something about it. Thank you.'

'She's a nurse, Maurice; she was the one who smelt the cyanide and pronounced him dead. And Denis Young's in a state – he was such a devout believer. For the sake of a lot of them I hope what almost happened to your niece isn't pointing to a scandal. Or another cliff jump.'

Phyllida heard the sigh. 'Don't bank on either.'

'I won't. Look, I must go; the man on the door'll be getting restive, and I've already been told off by Mr Dixon for my call to Peter.'

'Fine. See you eventually.'

It wasn't urgent, but before leaving, Phyllida performed the function for which her surroundings were designed, reflecting that a request for another visit within the next few hours might be viewed with suspicion and raise Mrs Santorini's profile to an undesirable public level. She emerged to the accompaniment of the noisy high flush that went with the flower-patterned

192

Victorian suite, looking forward to telling Peter, to his inevitable chagrin, that the downstairs cloakroom at Fifield Place was as handsome as the historic ablutions he treasured at the Agency and which he had dubbed the king of bathrooms.

Trolleys were being wheeled into the library as Phyllida and the uniform returned to it, and Phyllida noted with amusement the ease with which the stricken Bridgeites contrived to approach them and heap their plates with the excellent cold fare. Emotionally intact, she found herself extremely hungry and, until the edge was off her appetite, was impatient with the necessity of eating à l'Américaine with a fork alone. Mrs Henderson and Mr Dixon were notable exceptions to the general rush: Mrs Henderson showed no reaction whatsoever to the feast and Mr Dixon, when he had put a few bits on to a plate, brought up a small table, and placed it beside her chair with the plate upon it, sat down again without taking any food for himself.

'May I join you?' Mrs Santorini enquired of Roma, when they coincided by a trolley and Phyllida had noted with approval that Sally was approaching Denis.

'Sure.'

It was encouraging that Roma didn't wait for Colin when she had filled her plate, and led the way to a couple of chairs near the window, slightly removed from the main huddle.

'I'm so very sorry,' Mrs Santorini said, as they sat down.

'Yeah. It's a nightmare.'

'What you said to me just now, honey – about being sure your leader wouldn't have taken his life at the beginning of his talk – that sounds like sense to me. You'll say it to the police?'

'Why not?'

'Right. Roma ... you've a seeing eye, and a sharp brain. D'you have any idea who could have done this dreadful thing?'

'I'm afraid not.' But something wary had crossed the keen eyes before the response.

'Roma ... forgive me, but back home I'm a counsellor. I've been trained ... Just after it had happened ... I saw something in your face. A sort of grief. Real suffering, honey. And personal. I've a feeling it's something you can't explain to Colin.'

'You're wrong there, Peggie.' Roma seemed relaxed, even smiling her small triumph that Mrs Santorini had misread something.

'OK. But even so ... Look, honey, I'm back across the Atlantic next week. Sometimes it's easiest to talk to strangers.'

'I know.' Roma dropped her eyes to her lap, gave a deep sigh, and looked up at Phyllida with another smile. 'So what the hell? There's no girlfriend I'm going to tell. I

194

craved Charles Henderson like addicts crave crack.'

'Oh! Roma! And he craved you?'

'Along with a host of others. I suppose I just about stood out from the crowd. But that didn't stop him wanting other women – or taking them – and they let themselves be taken, except for that girl this morning; and one or two earlier failures. That I know of. Boys, too. He wasn't fussy. He just had this massive sexual ego. I think it was the idea of mastery as much as an itchy tool. Oh, yeah, I fascinated him; he always wanted me. But if I wasn't around, if I was never to be around again, he'd have coped.'

'Oh, Roma. I'm so sorry. But knowing what you do about him, how could you have...'

'I've often wondered. Wished I could be released. Thought I'd managed it, and then the next time ... Isn't it in *Othello?* "I know a lady in Venice would have walked barefoot to Palestine for a touch of his nether lip." That was me.'

'But Colin...'

'This is just for you. This is *all* just for you.'

'Of course, honey.' It wouldn't be Peggie Santorini who would talk to the police.

'Colin and I *are* close, but not in the way we hope it seems. Colin's gay. He doesn't want to come out; he's an engineer and it

wouldn't fit. So we're together in public –
and like to be – and in private, I'm my way,
and he's his.'

'Colin ... and Mr Henderson?'

'God, no! Colin's homosexual, not de-
praved.'

'I see. Well...'

'You don't see, Peggie. How could you?'

'Does anyone else in The Bridge know?
Your young friends...'

'Nobody knows – except you, now. Nobody.'

'Roma ... you'll be talking to the police in
a moment. Mr Henderson's dead. Don't
you think you ought to tell them ... something? If you don't say anything, don't tell
them about the things he did, someone
might literally get away with murder.'

It was academic, of course: before the day
was out the Detective Chief Superintendent
would know everything that Roma had just
confided to Mrs Santorini, but he could do
more with it if it was in Roma's own statement.

'And there's another thing, honey. You say
nobody knows what you've just told me.
Now, I wouldn't be so sure. Mr Dixon, for a
start. He's got a kind of an all-seeing eye.
And a man's wife ... I guess you're in a bit of
a cloud cuckoo land if you really believe
you've kept your secret, and if you don't tell
it to the police I've an idea someone else

196

will, and less favourably than you can tell it yourself. So talk to them, Roma. Let them see that there's nothing you need to hide.'

If there was, Kendrick might just catch a glimpse of it.

Twelve

'Sit down, please, Mr Dixon. Now, let me start by saying how sorry I am this dreadful thing has happened to your ... to your leader. I gather that you are business manager to ... to The Bridge' – DS Wetherhead was aware of the slight shudder that passed through the long body at his side – 'and so I'm afraid you must be the one to tell us the details of the arrangements for Mr Henderson's talk today. For a start, who filled the carafe and set it on the table in the library? And who would have had access to it both in there, and before it was put in place? Take your time.'

'I have no difficulty answering those questions, Chief Superintendent, Sergeant.' The steady grey eyes moved from Kendrick to his sergeant and back again. 'Half an hour or so before the audience began to assemble – before I took up my place at the library door – I took a carafe and a glass from a kitchen cupboard, filled the carafe with water from the cold tap, put them on a small tray and carried them through to the sanctum. I would probably have taken them straight into the library and put them on the table where they were when Mr Henderson drank, but when I said I was going to fetch the water, he told me he had a slight sore throat and wanted a drink before he went into the library.'

'And did you see him have one?'

'No. I left him immediately; I had things to attend to. When I went back about twenty minutes later, he told me he'd had a sip – I think he used that word – so clearly the water at that point was uncontaminated. I carried glass and carafe out to the table in the library. I noted that the level in the carafe had gone down very slightly.'

'You're a close observer, sir,' DS Wetherhead commented.

'As always. The library was filling up by the time I set the tray down, and it was by no means the focus of attention during the five or ten minutes before everyone was seated.' For the first time the steady voice hesitated. 'I have to say that anyone could have lifted the glass and slipped something into the carafe without being noticed.'

'Thank you for your admirably clear statement, Mr Dixon.' Kendrick and his sergeant exchanged a brief expressionless glance, but each could read in the other's face the sense of weariness engendered by the reluctantly acquired knowledge that most people in Fifield Place that morning could have brought about Charles Henderson's death – including Charles Henderson himself.

'So Mr Henderson could have taken his preliminary sip,' Kendrick went on, 'and then poisoned either the glass or the carafe – or both.'

'He could.'

'And do you believe it possible that he did, Mr Dixon?'

'If he had drunk the water at the climax of his speech, I would have had little doubt, Mr Kendrick, distressing though it is to think that the man who forbade anticipation of the afterlife should have been guilty of the sin himself.' It was impossible, Kendrick thought glumly, to observe distress in Mr Dixon, or any other emotion. 'As it was ... I cannot conceive of our leader being murdered, so I must believe that when his throat continued to hurt – it was audible in his voice – he poured a drink as a reflex gesture, forgetting what he had done to it ... No,' Mr Dixon continued with a thin smile, as the two policemen gazed at him impassively, 'it doesn't sound convincing; but nor does the idea that someone killed so noble a man.'

A man that Dixon had to know had

behaved ignobly with countless young women. But there might be an entirely different motive for murder.

'The parents of the boy who jumped over the cliff, Mr Dixon – are they here today?'

'No. And I don't know if he had parents. *You* will know, Mr Kendrick, from your investigation of his death, that he lived alone.'

'Yes ... He must have had friends, though; and there were his fellow members ... However, we're assembling facts at the moment, and you have been of considerable help to us. Though you haven't mentioned that Mr Henderson's sister came into his sanctum shortly before he emerged to address his followers – via the hidden door from the back hall, which she told us about, and which nobody but you and the family and the house staff know about. You must have seen her; she says she saw you.'

'Yes ... I'm sorry, it slipped my mind...' It was the first time either policeman had seen Mr Dixon less than fully composed; and the first time both were certain he was lying. 'Yes ... I left them and went back into the library as she was telling him she wanted to close the chapel and not let anyone in after lunch. She was just being vindictive, Mr Kendrick, hoping to upset our leader's concentration before he addressed us. Miss Henderson is not a member of The Bridge –

which I presume she also told you.'

'I think she told the whole company, Mr Dixon. So she was alone with her brother just before he came out to speak. Were the carafe and the glass still in the sanctum while she was there, or had you brought them into the library by then? Mr Dixon?'

'I ... I'm trying to remember. I know when I went back into the sanctum a few moments later she had gone back down the secret passage. It was a very brief visit and I can't be sure which side of it I removed the water tray. I'm sorry, Chief Superintendent. I'll continue trying to remember.'

'If you will, sir,' DS Wetherhead said. 'It could be important. Did Mrs Henderson visit her husband in the sanctum while the carafe and glass were there?'

Mr Dixon moved his head slightly, and Kendrick saw a bead of sweat descending his temple. 'That I don't know, Chief Superintendent.' Again, the strong voice had faltered. 'He and she usually spend a few moments together just before he speaks to the members in the De Luxe, but this is the first time we have had a Bridge meeting at the house. So there is no precedent here.'

'I understand. But it would have been possible for her to pay her husband a visit at the last moment that no one was aware of? She could have gone in and out of the door in the back hall without being observed?'

'Yes. She could. But there was so little time...'

'Thank you, Mr Dixon. We shall no doubt be speaking to you again, but for now, thank you.'

'Chief Superintendent...'

DS Wetherhead stayed the hand he had stretched towards the tape switch.

'Yes, Mr Dixon?'

'The smell of the cyanide – like almond essence ... It was strong and I smelt it. The fact that it didn't stop Mr Henderson from drinking – that could suggest he knew the cyanide was in the water and was expecting to smell it.'

'Indicating suicide. That point will not be overlooked, Mr Dixon; but nor will the fact – we've already been led to believe it's a fact – that Mr Henderson was in an abnormally excitable state and could therefore have drunk the poisoned water before becoming aware of its not-to-be-expected smell.'

'Yes. Of course.'

'Sergeant Withers has set up shop in the dining room, and he'll take your statement there.'

'Yes. Just one more thing, Mr Kendrick...'

'Yes?'

'Can you answer me one question? Did Mrs Henderson tell you that she visited her husband in the sanctum shortly before he emerged to address us?'

Kendrick studied the continuingly impassive face while he considered whether to grant the request, and decided to do so. 'No, Mr Dixon, she did not. She told us that the last time she saw her husband was before he entered the sanctum.'

'Thank you. I believe she was telling the truth.'

'So what did you make of that, sir?' Fred Wetherhead enquired as the door closed behind the business manager.

'Plenty of possible facts, Fred, but a vital one unoffered and an accursed self-control. Anyway, some facts about Dixon himself, proven accurate, will soon be coming in. We already know he doesn't have a record.'

'And we already know that pretty well anyone here today could have bumped the master off. Strange how the wife is so sure someone did, and the manager so sure someone didn't. Special pleading in one or both cases?'

'That's what we've got to find out, Fred. In the meantime ... I'm inclined to think the reluctance of Dixon's corroboration of Miss Henderson's visit, and his conviction that Mrs Henderson didn't pay one, is as interesting vis-à-vis him as it is vis-à-vis them. He hadn't forgotten for a moment about the sister's visit, and I've an idea he knows that she and the carafe were in the sanctum at the same time. It's as if he's trying to protect them.'

'At his own expense. Yes, sir, very odd.'

'Altruism isn't a characteristic I would associate with Dixon; but loyalty, perhaps ... They are the master's family, after all.'

'That's true, sir. The sister ... She did tell us herself about her visit, and appeared very open in every way. I suppose saying there were times she could have murdered him just might have been a double bluff, but that would mean she was devious enough to make herself seem the soul of honesty and it's hard to imagine another Miss Moon.'

'It is indeed, Fred. On the other hand, though, Hermione Henderson has a very powerful motive for wishing her brother out of the way. In a joint tenancy the death of one owner puts the whole property, or whatever, immediately into the hands of the other. And Henderson *was* agitating to put the chapel into Bridgeite hands.'

'Very true, sir. Maurice...'

Kendrick was aware of his sergeant shifting in his seat. Always to his puzzled amusement, the only time Fred Wetherhead used his first name, apart from when they were off duty, was when he was embarrassed. 'What is it, Fred?'

'The ... er ... the sex angle, sir. Your niece's experience – well, near experience. We haven't got on to it with either Dixon or Mrs Henderson. I was expecting you to—'

'Don't worry, Fred, I will. But I'm hoping Miss Roma Westlake will broach the subject for me, which, if Miss Moon has anything to do with it, she will. If she doesn't, and if I can't get her to, then I'll have to quote an unnameable source of information.' Not Sam, if he could help it. Kendrick was suddenly and reluctantly aware that his hope of a revelation from Miss Westlake was motivated as much by his desire to keep his niece out of it as by his professional expectations. 'In any event, Fred, I felt it was a bit early, so far as Mrs Henderson is concerned, to bring up the subject of her husband's attempt at infidelity on the day of his death. We can always promote second interviews. And third and fourth. And, having examined the principals in some detail, we'll hope to go pretty speedily through the chorus.'

'Sir.'

'Mrs Henderson's apparent confidence that her husband didn't take his own life appears to be buoying her up at the moment – if it isn't an attempt to deflect attention from a killing she carried out herself – but if it's genuine, it's unlikely to last, and when the balloon deflates, it's bound to emit some air.'

'I wonder why she's so sure – if she really is, as you say.'

'If we're lucky, it'll be because she already knows his interest in his young acolytes has a sexual element, and sees a potential murderer among his conquests or would-be conquests – which knowledge, by the same token, could mean she sneaked down the passage and poisoned his water carafe herself; and I really can't believe, Fred, that the master carried on with other girls the way he tried to carry on with Sam, and managed to keep it entirely to himself.' Kendrick glanced at his watch. 'Miss Moon has had well over an hour. Let's ask for Miss Westlake.'

With the removal of the body and the release from the library, following their interviews, of Miss Henderson, Mrs Henderson and Mr Dixon, Phyllida was aware of a slight relaxation of the stricken atmosphere. Once the initial outrage and disbelief had been bawled forth, voices had dropped to a whisper punctuated by wary glances at the screens and the principal mourners, and it was clearly something of a relief to all to be free of the sight of Mrs Henderson's mute grief and Mr Dixon's sombre inscrutability, to say nothing of the sister's flouncing fury. Some of the seats had edged back towards the centre of the room, and Phyllida even heard a shrill female laugh, quickly stifled.

She and Sally were comparing whispered notes when Roma was summoned to the sanctum. She drifted past Phyllida and Sally with a lingering smile that gave no indication of the effect on her of Mrs Santorini's advice. 'Courage, honey,' Mrs Santorini breathed.

Most of the food had been eaten, and someone had pushed the trolleys towards the door. Movement and intermingling had begun, although still restricted to just over half the room, and several people were standing at the windows and staring wistfully at the long, tranquil view. Phyllida supposed they must be feeling like she and Sally had just discovered they both felt: that it had all happened a long time ago, that they had always known it would happen – a common, illogical reaction to an unforeseen tragedy, she had learned from both her own experience and the experience of other people; whereas her heralded loss of Jack was always in the present, and he remained as close to her as he had been in the moment before she had lost him...

'What a long day!' Sally sighed as she looked at her watch. 'And it's still only three o'clock! I wonder when they'll call *us* in?'

'At the bitter end, to give us as much time as possible to conduct our own interviews. Cheer up, though; I don't think they'll be talking for more than a very few moments to the general membership and the staff. But we ought to get back to work. Well, I ought:

I'm on a job.'

'To which you've recruited *me*. I'll have another go at Denis; we were interrupted the first time I tried, and anyway, he seemed to be still in shock. Marian's all tears and nothing useful, I decided. What about you?'

'I think I'll try Tom and Felicity. They're so wrapped up in one another they might manage a degree of objectivity. Then Charlie ... This is the sort of occasion, Sally, where I'm glad Mrs Santorini's American.'

'Colin should be interesting.'

'You're right. I'll begin with him. Sorry, leader's privilege.'

'OK. He was watching you and Roma talking, by the way. He might suspect she was confiding in you. Or she might even have said something; they've had their heads together since.'

'Yes. Well, if she did, I suspect Colin's controlled enough to keep it to himself, if he wants to.'

Mrs Santorini had scarcely made a languid descent into the chair beside him, however, when he turned to her with the first real smile Phyllida had seen on his face.

'Peggie Santorini! Roma was just telling me about the advice you gave her.'

'After she had confided in me, Colin.'

'And she confided, I gather, because you saw something in her grief you read as more than shock and horror at the loss of a leader.

Are you a mind-reader?'

'I'm a counsellor back home; I told Roma that.'

'Ah, yes. Roma told me she trusted you to keep our secret, by the way. I hope her trust will be justified.'

'It will, Colin. Peggie Santorini won't breathe a word of it. As for my advice, I'm convinced it was good, or I wouldn't have offered it. I'm not a busybody.'

'You're certainly not in busybody mould.' Colin's searching look seemed to take in Mrs Santorini's inner as well as her outer self, and Phyllida experienced the frisson that overcame her on the rare occasions she was afraid her character might not be disguise enough. The look was admiring as well as penetrative, but it was an admiration one might feel for a picture or other work of art, and she welcomed her sudden amusement, overcoming the fear, at finding herself regretful that Colin's charm would never be intimately enjoyed by a woman.

'I hope the Enabler's death isn't going to make life difficult for you and Roma personally,' Peggie said. 'I felt that Roma telling the police what she knows would make that less likely and be very much kinder to your nerves than letting the police find things out for themselves.'

'Which they would. Yep. Oh, I think your advice was good, Peggie – especially as it

209

included the suggestion that she leave me out of it.'

'Well, Colin, I gathered from Roma that the police have nothing to find out about you – that your role vis-à-vis Mr Henderson was quite negative, if you will excuse the word.'

'I welcome it.'

'Do you think the Enabler could possibly have taken his own life?'

'I don't know.' *And don't sound all that interested*; but Phyllida had already suspected that The Bridge was as much an expedient for Colin as it was for Roma. 'Roma could have got it right: if he'd waited to drink until he'd had his say, it would have been a possibility.'

'But that would have been a dreadful precedent for his followers, wouldn't it? Doing what he had so strictly forbidden?'

'Maybe his activities had started to catch up with him. If he was dead, he wouldn't be worrying about them, or about flouting his own dogma. But who knows? How long did you tell Roma you'll be staying in Seaminster?'

A few facts politely exchanged about Peggie's immediate plans and Colin's business life, and Mrs Santorini graciously excused herself with the plea that she ought to touch base with young Sally.

'Denis is in an awful state!' Sally exclaimed, in an undertone that Phyllida suggested she should further modify. 'He seems to be more upset – well, ideologically. He's as much concerned for The Bridge itself as for its fallen hero.'

'A true believer. I suspected it from the start, just as I suspected Roma had other axes to grind. Marian and Charlie are probably true believers as well, though with Marian I suppose there could be an element of hero-worship; but I can't see any of the people here today, Sally, apart from Roma and Colin, being involved in The Bridge to get anything more out of it than spiritual sustenance.'

'Except Mr Dixon, perhaps.'

'My other exception too. I wonder how Maurice is getting on with him. Immovable object and irresistible force. I wish I could have been a fly on the wall at *that* interview.'

'He's the only interviewee so far not to have come back into the library. Phyllida – sorry, Peggie – there has to be another way out of that inside room.'

'Of course. And it's a nice warm feeling to know the Chief Superintendent will be telling us about it. Sally, you really are perceptive. I wish you'd consider another career.'

'And waste my exams? Oh, I love doing this – I've been on the most exquisite high ever since I put my wig on – but ... I love

211

being a librarian. I feel awfully torn.'

'A luxury not given to many on the employment front. Well, we shall just have to recruit you for specific duties.'

'The best of both worlds. By the way, I think Miss Lubbock and I ought to call on Denis this evening. If we get away from here.'

'So do I. But how will Jeremy react to another night without you?'

'I've prepared him; so that if I did go home, he'd see it as an unexpected bonus. D'you think we *will* get away?'

'Yes. They're getting through them pretty fast now, and policemen as well as public need breaks. If they don't finish before dark, I think they'll settle for resuming in the morning. D'you want Charlie, or would you rather take Tom and Felicity?'

'Do you really have to ask?'

'All right, honey. I'll take Charlie. Another leader privilege. Rough with the smooth.'

Charlie was sitting alone, scowling at the fireplace, as Mrs Santorini drew a chair up beside her.

'Charlie! I have your name right, haven't I?'

A sullen stare. 'It's what I'm known as.'

'Yes ... Charlie, I'm so very sorry about what's happened. People are saying all sorts of different things. Do *you* believe your leader could have taken his own life?'

212

'Never! The man – the more than man – who tells us each time he honours us with his presence that we must wait our due time for our apotheosis. It's a wicked, wicked suggestion. It's come from that Roma, I suppose.'

'It's come from a number of people.'

'So you're going round quizzing the membership, Mrs...'

'Santorini. Peggie.' A frisson again, of a different kind – she must stay within her apparent parameters. 'Of course not, Charlie. But back home I'm a counsellor, and I'm always a bit nosey about people's motives for their behaviour. It's gotten to be a habit.'

'Humph. Well, our Enabler wasn't *people;* he was something more. Now, if you'll excuse me, I really don't feel like talking at the moment.'

'I understand. I'm sorry I disturbed you. I can assure you I'm upset myself. I've only just learned about The Bridge, as you know, but I was very much hoping for enlightenment from your leader.'

'Yes ... well...' Charlie was the one person she had met who was immune to Mrs Santorini's charm, but Phyllida believed her to be fair and suspected her of being a lot less tough than she at first appeared, if approached in the right way.

'So how were Tom and Felicity?' she

enquired of Sally when they were standing together at a window, watching white cloud moving across a blue sky, and she had given her report on Charlie.

'Still engrossed with one another, but I think genuinely shocked and upset. Can't believe their leader could have taken his own life, in view of all he's said to them about the wickedness of suicide, but can't believe either that anyone would have murdered him.'

'So they say,' Phyllida murmured. 'So everyone no doubt says. Sally, I'm just learning how difficult a job Maurice Kendrick has.'

'Looks as if he's ready for you,' Sally responded. 'Here comes his sergeant.'

'Mrs Santorini?' Fred Wetherhead said deferentially. 'If you'd like to come with me. I'm sorry we've had to keep you waiting so long. You won't have to wait much longer now, madam,' he said to Sally, unable, Phyllida noted to her amusement, to suppress all curiosity from his face.

'No tape yet, Fred,' Kendrick reminded him, when Phyllida was seated across the table from them and his sergeant was stretching his hand out towards the machine.

'Sorry, sir. Reflex.'

'We'll devise a brief interview with Mrs Santorini before Miss Moon leaves. But first

... I'm sorry it's been such a long day, Phyllida, but I know you won't have been wasting it.'

'I hope not. Roma?'

'The bizarre triangle of herself, the Enabler, and Colin Heard. I presume that sums up her confession to you.'

'Yes. Oh, I'm so glad, Maurice.'

'There was a bit more. She told us she was watching the door into the secret passage a quarter of an hour or so before the official proceedings began, wondering if she could snatch a few moments with the master; but she didn't try, because she saw his wife going in.'

Thirteen

Kendrick released everyone in the house at just before seven o'clock, soon after DS Wetherhead had closed the sanctum door on the last person to occupy the Queen Anne chair that had faced them for the past six hours across the Queen Anne table: the youth the gardener had presented to them as his lad.

Kendrick went out to the library personally to tell everyone they could at last go home, and said nothing about further interviews. In any event, the people for whom he was certain this information was relevant had already dispersed to other parts of the house. Kendrick had learned from a reluctant Mr Dixon that a bedroom was permanently at his disposal in Fifield Place, which, in the light of Steve's report of following the business manager and the leader there at the end of their last town meeting, he had expected.

The only restriction he placed on the roomful of remaining suspects was the general injunction that, unless they had informed him during their interviews that they were due to leave the area within the next few days, he would expect them to remain at home or to notify the police, if the advisability of going away suddenly presented itself.

'Thank you for your patience,' he concluded. 'I can assure you that as much information as possible will be released to the public as our investigation of this unfortunate affair proceeds.'

In such highly charged company Kendrick regretted his under-description of the death of Charles Henderson the second he had uttered it, and was not surprised at its shrieked repetition by the only member of The Bridge not sitting or standing still, but pausing now in his striding up and down beside the windows to glare at Kendrick and his sergeant, fists clenched at his sides.

'Unfortunate and tragic for you all,' Kendrick corrected smoothly, acknowledging Denis Young's outburst by no more than a second adjective, and agreeably aware that it had come from the one person in the room, apart from Sally Hargreaves, with whom Phyllida Moon was likely to be in personal contact the near side of bedtime.

'Denis is in a high old state,' Sally said, as she negotiated the drive. 'We'll have to do something about him tonight, won't we?'

'Yes; but I think we'll wait a while, because I've an idea he'll be doing something about us. I can't see his young friends being in the mood to assemble in the Heights at the end of a day like this, and anyway, I see him more in the role of inviter than invitee. Poor Denis!'

'I know. He really believed. D'you think it'll go on? The Bridge?'

'I don't see how. Oh, I expect some of its members will go on being convinced something happened and that they really did make contact with someone dead, but I can't see them getting together – well, not in the long term. I suppose there could be a few meetings, but they'll be such uncharismatic affairs they'll soon peter out. Apart from Denis, I feel concerned for Marian and Charlie, but I think the others will survive pretty well intact. Of those we've met at least – we don't know anything about the rest of the membership, do we?'

'They'll probably find another minority group to latch on to,' Sally said dismissively. 'Some people are always looking for something spiritually special, and often it seems as if the smaller the better. Big fish in a little pond. But if it's been told the secret of the universe, why does it stay so small?'

'Because it's born of nothing more than a skewed imagination, I suppose. Look, Sally, it sounds tedious, but I think we'd both better stay in character until pretty well into the night in case Denis Young comes knocking.'

'And if he doesn't – we go to him?'

'We ring him if we don't hear from him, but I suggest not before about ten o'clock. It'll feel like a long wait, and those trolleys seem a long way in the past. Let's stop for fish and chips, take it home, and open a bottle.'

'And eat and drink by that fascinating window.' Phyllida felt the snuggle of contentment beside her, and was reminded that for Sally there could be nothing in her new role of assistant PI that she would find boring or routine.

'Of course.'

Both women discovered they were famished as they unwrapped the oil-soaked papers and the delicious smells arose, and Sally had made a big inroad into her chips with her fingers by the time Phyllida had assembled plates and cutlery. They dragged the apology for a dining table over to the window, with two upright chairs, watching the lights spring up to defy the descending dark as they silently satisfied their hunger.

'It must be fun to live in a really upmarket high-rise, like Canary Wharf,' Sally said on her last mouthful. 'So long as you weren't there all the time. A pad there and a small place in the country would be perfect.'

'But you'd miss Seaminster.' Phyllida wiped some of the grease away with one of the paper napkins that had awaited them in an unopened packet in a kitchen drawer.

'Maybe. I don't know. One thing I do know, though, is that I'm longing to see Denis.' Sally got to her feet and put the empty plates together. 'But I'm glad he didn't interrupt *that*. Coffee? Or another glass of wine?'

'Better make it coffee; with luck our working day isn't over yet.'

They had moved to the so-called easy chairs, and had almost finished their coffee when there was a prolonged peal on the front doorbell.

'Miss Lubbock's still indisposed,' Phyllida said quickly, as Sally sprang to her feet. 'Mrs Santorini came back with you for supper and you were on the point of driving her back to the hotel but there's no hurry ... Go and let him in.'

The bell pealed again before Sally reached the front door, and when she opened it Denis Young almost fell against her in the narrow passage.

'Denis! Whatever is the matter?'

'D'you really have to ask? You were there, weren't you?'

'Well, yes, I was ... and of course it was awful. For goodness sake come in and sit down. Peggie's come back with me; I was just about to drive her back to the Golden Lion, but there's no hurry. Miss Lubbock's still in bed, I'm afraid, but she's feeling better. Come on through to the lounge.' Denis was moving like a sleepwalker, and Sally found herself guiding him. 'There you are. Sit down.'

She half-pushed him into the armchair she had just left, and sat down on the upright chair beside it. Peggie was on her feet and staring at him with concern.

'What on earth is it, honey? You look terrible. Where have you been since we were all let go?'

'Driving around. Walking.' The angry, bloodshot eyes glared at her.

'Have you eaten?' Mrs Santorini asked.

'Eaten?' It was like the repetition of the word 'handbag' by a good actress in *The*

Importance of Being Earnest. 'Food would choke me.' Disapprovingly he sniffed the air. 'I can tell *you* both managed some.'

It was the impoliteness rather than the histrionics that convinced Phyllida that Denis Young was truly devastated. 'We managed something,' she said, daring Sally to smile. 'We were exhausted after such a terrible day, and we just tried to put a bit of strength back. Perhaps you'd like some tea or coffee, at least, Denis?'

'I'll have a glass of water. Thanks' – as Sally sped off. 'I'm sorry,' he muttered to Mrs Santorini. 'To barge in like this and then be so rude. I hardly know what I'm doing or saying. The Enabler ... and people suggesting that he took his own life! It's obscene!'

'How and why Mr Henderson died will come to light, Denis; the police will make sure of that.'

'And his message will die too; I know what people are like. Out of sight, out of mind. But it won't die with me. The Enabler gave me my friend, and I'll never lose him!'

'Of course you won't, Denis.'

'And you've got to think on,' Sally said in the doorway, glass in hand, 'like Roma said in your flat when Stan died ...You're the one who's suffering; the Enabler's safely crossed the Bridge.'

'That's right,' Mrs Santorini agreed, while

Phyllida thanked Sally silently for reminding Denis, as she had been unable to, of the solace Roma had offered for the death of Stan Dolby when his other non-Bridgeite visitor had been Miss Lubbock.

Denis's blotched face lightened for an instant, and when the light faded, Phyllida fancied the despair that settled back on it was not quite as total as it had been before.

'Yes. I know that. And I know I ought to feel glad for him. But – well, it leaves us all so ... so *lonely!*' The whining voice petered out in a wail, and to Sally's obvious embarrassment Denis bent his head to his knees and began to cry.

Phyllida's reaction was a moment of empathy with the sad young man in front of her, the new life, new importance, new hope, sucked out of him. Sally meanwhile, quickly mastering her reflex, was managing to look grave and to stretch out a hand to pat a heaving shoulder.

Neither woman spoke while Denis Young wept, and after a few moments he felt for an off-colour handkerchief, blew his nose and pulled himself upright.

'I'm sorry, I'm OK now. I know you're right about the Enabler: he's safe. It's The Bridge I'm concerned about, and ... and ... all the people...'

And yourself, Phyllida finished for him silently. Because what would he do? Being a clerk in an office with little or no personal life would once have been all he knew, but after his hour of glory he must be looking on the resumption of his pre-Bridge routine with horror...

'I'm going to make you some toast, honey,' Mrs Santorini said decisively. 'Whatever you say, you've got to keep your strength up. Do you prefer tea or coffee?'

'Thanks, I'll have tea. Two sugars. Thanks.'

Denis ate and drank without apparent difficulty, to the accompaniment of would-be soothing dialogue between the women, and slowly appeared to be regaining some hold of himself; but his offer to drive Mrs Santorini back to the Golden Lion was so listless it was easily overcome, and he left them promising to obey their chorused injunction to go straight to bed. He even managed to send his best wishes to Miss Lubbock and his hopes of seeing her before long, but when they had closed the front door on him and were listening to his plodding tread diminishing down the corridor, Phyllida voiced her concern.

'I do hope he doesn't do anything foolish. He's bound to have thought about Stan Dolby...'

'I know. But surely ... Oh, he wouldn't do *that*. I mean ... you'd have to be seriously off your head to jump over a cliff.'

'Perhaps he is.'

'Well ... anyway, you can do something about a lot of things, Phyllida, but even you can't do anything about that!'

'No ... So I'll say goodnight to Mrs Santorini, and to you Sally, and get to my bed.'

Detective Chief Superintendent Kendrick did not sleep well. His relief to be facing the Bridgeites as a policeman rather than as an apprehensive relative of a potential victim was still strong, but he was unable to banish the faces of his three chief suspects from his mind's eye, and when he eventually managed to doze off they became the targets in a shooting gallery, heads and shoulders passing in relentless loopline in front of the rifle he was unable to lift, let alone fire, the face of the dead man's wife, in the second before it disappeared, transforming into a mask of terror. It was a bad dream that by its third or fourth rerun had turned into a nightmare from which he woke sweating and muttering.

'That was bad, by the sound of it,' Miriam murmured. 'You should be having happy dreams, with Sam safe.'

'I know. It's just ... There's a fluffy little lady who could be a cold-blooded killer, and tomorrow I've got to tackle her.'

'And if she isn't, she's just a fluffy little lady ... Yes, I see. No other candidates?' Bed was the only place Miriam ever asked questions about a case in progress that Maurice hadn't chosen to discuss with her, and the evening had been taken up with relief over Sam and telephone chats with her and Mary.

'Yes. About fifty. Realistically, though, certainly another two: the sister and the business manager.'

Kendrick felt the shudder beside him. 'How terrible to have the people nearest to you, the people you presumably love, and certainly rely on, likely to have been your killers.'

'Only one, I think. I can't envisage a conspiracy. So it's not quite as awful as it sounds. But that fluffy little lady who's just become a widow ... if she's innocent I could be about to destroy her.'

'Maurice ... once upon a time I don't believe that would have worried you. I've an idea you're becoming more compassionate in your old age. I like it.'

'Dear God, I hope not.' But he was laughing as he pulled her to him.

He was not laughing when he and DS Wetherhead faced each other across his desk at half past eight the next morning. When he had first sat down he had swivelled his chair for the solace of the long sea view, sombre today under dramatic whorls of cloud fading from dark grey to light grey to a shrinking bank of white just above the thin line of the horizon. DS Wetherhead, whom he had encountered in the outer office and whose presence he had invited with a nod of the head, had followed him into his private office and sat in respectful silence until his chief had looked his fill.

'So, Fred,' Kendrick said, as he swung reluctantly to face his sergeant, 'where do we go from here? When can we expect the forensic report?'

'They've told me soon after nine. They worked devotedly late last night, sir.' DS Wetherhead had learned over the years to offer an implicit caution to his chief against expecting too much too soon, and had perfected the art of delivering it in the lightest of tones.

'I'm sure, Fred, and I appreciate it' – point taken yet again, and the two men exchanged slight smiles of understanding. 'I'll be glad of the excuse of some information to impart – well, at least corroborate – when I go back to Mrs Henderson.'

'That should certainly make it easier, sir. And I've been thinking ... If we have another word with Dixon first, we can find out from him how she's standing up to it all. And with official information about the poison...'

'We'll be in a position to find out how likely or unlikely it was that any or all of the

226

members of our chief-suspect trio could have got hold of it. So with luck it'll be the next half-hour, Fred, that will be the longest part of the day.'

In the event it was forty-five minutes – a forty-five minutes during which Fred Wetherhead wished, not for the first time, that his Chief could find temporary solace in crossword puzzles or computer patience as well as his sea view.

By a quarter to ten they were on their way back to Fifield Place, Kendrick driving and definitive information on the cause of Charles Henderson's death set out on a sheet of paper inside the thin briefcase on DS Wetherhead's lap.

'I think we'll invite Mr Dixon to tell us about himself,' Kendrick said, as they drove into real countryside. The early cloud had lifted and lightened, and there was a concentrated glow behind the thin cover to the south-east, suggesting that the sun might soon break through. Kendrick had his first sight of the brilliance of the newly shooting green among the dark twigs of the hawthorn hedges to each side of them, which was his annual reassurance that the leaves and the blossoms of spring were on their way. 'Wife, and sister even more if she's what she seems, are open books compared to the man of mystery, and it's damned hard to get information about people who have never been in trouble with the police.' But Kendrick's tone was more relaxed than his words, and DS Wetherhead was relieved to hear a low, unidentifiable humming sound coming from his chief as they drove on, which ceased only as the car curved with the drive and Fred saw the sternness of the DCS's profile; but Kendrick, he reflected, had always hated poisons with a particular hatred and thought no penalty severe enough for anyone who had killed in that calculating way. Whereas, Fred's thoughts continued, his chief had always regretted harsh sentences for the *crime passionel*, where the murderer had known his or her victim and been carried away by misery rather than by greed or fear...

'So here we are again, Fred.' Kendrick blinked as he got out of the car and found that the sun had made it through the cloud, albeit a pastel sun bestowing no more than a gentle warmth on his cheeks as he stood for a moment outside the house and admired its proportions.

'Chief Inspector!'

Brian Dixon was descending a set of steps; he must have been standing in the doorway as impatiently as Kendrick had so lately stood at his office window, waiting for what he ... dreaded? ... simply wanted to get over with? ... was apprehensive about on behalf of Charles Henderson's wife, if his reactions of the day before really pointed to what Kendrick had thought he had seen in them? It was impossible still to see this man as anything but an enigma.

Yet Dixon was smiling as he reached the policemen and held out his hand to Kendrick. 'Good morning!' The hand was cool, dry and firm. 'Please come inside. And Sergeant Wetherhead.'

'How is Mrs Henderson this morning?' DS Wetherhead enquired, when they had taken up their positions of the day before and Mr Dixon was facing them across the handsome table.

'I haven't seen her myself, but I'm told she accepted some tea in her room an hour or so ago when it was offered. I called the doctor last night, a little against Mrs Henderson's will, I'm afraid, and he gave her something to ease her. Not that anything really can, Mr Kendrick.'

'Of course not. I'm only sorry that we must talk to her again, but she was seen entering the passage that leads to the room off the library just before your meeting proper began.' Kendrick had debated with himself long and hard over whether to give this information to Dixon before reminding Mrs Henderson of it, and had decided that Dixon's reaction would be worth observing and that it would be possible to ensure that he and Mrs Henderson did not encounter

229

one another, alone or in company, between his interview and hers. 'You are aware that she denied having visited her husband when he was in this room before coming out to the library.'

'Ah!' There was no doubt that the grey face had grown more ashen, and that there was alarm in the deep-set grey eyes. 'That is a shock to me, Mr Kendrick.' But the steady eyes had veered briefly away from his, and Kendrick was convinced that the business manager was lying and that his shock had come from the revelation that the police shared his knowledge of the visit rather than from the fact that it had taken place. 'But I can assure you that Mrs Henderson will have withheld the information from you simply because she wished to avoid being questioned about something completely innocent.'

'I hope you're right, Mr Dixon, but you will know that we are unable simply to accept your assurance; we have to establish the truth or untruth of everything that is said to us when we are investigating a crime. It has taken the police very little time to discover that Mr Henderson was not monogamous. It's difficult to believe that you – and Mr Henderson's wife – were unaware of this ... I'm wondering if you might wish to alter anything in your statement.'

'Certainly not, Chief Superintendent!'

Dixon was managing to look mildly but genuinely affronted. 'I do not know whether or not Mrs Henderson visited her husband in the sanctum shortly before he came into the library, and I stand by that statement. And ... Mr Henderson is – was – a man of many gifts and many ... requirements. None of which, I am confident, broke the law.'

'Thank you for sharing your views with us, Mr Dixon. Now, I hope, you will share some information on the subject of yourself. It would be helpful if you could let us have a verbal curriculum vitae. We know nothing of how you come to be in the position of business manager to this ... this movement, or of the qualifications and experience that caused the position to be offered to you. We will learn your personal history one way or another, so I think it would be to your advantage to tell us about it yourself.'

'My late wife was a cousin of the Hendersons,' Dixon offered, with an ironic smile, 'and when Charles decided he wanted – how can I put it? – to market his newly discovered powers, he contacted me. If the word "nepotism" springs to mind, you may start to think that my qualifications and experience didn't feature very largely in the decision to appoint me. In fact that would not be true. Mr Henderson did much that he did instinctively, but his wife is a clear-sighted realist, and I think she would have dissuaded him from appointing me had I not had the right sort of background. When they contacted me, I was bringing my career in the City to a premature close – owing to a heart problem – but I am still a non-executive director of two companies...' Mr Dixon had drawn a sheet of paper towards him, and had started to write in a small, speedy hand.

'You believed in Mr Henderson's powers? You saw an alternative – and probably less stressful – source of income? Both?'

Another thin smile. 'I don't have to answer your first question, Mr Kendrick. As for the second ... I didn't – I still don't – see a serious source of income. I retired very comfortably, and what I saw was an intriguing situation, with a chance to study human nature face to face with – I won't call it demagogy, gentlemen, because Mr Henderson's motives, at least, were benign, but with an abnormally seductive message. And I thought ... who knew? Another messiah?'

'And are you able to tell us? Was yesterday a second crucifixion?'

Kendrick heard Fred Wetherhead's shocked hiss of breath as he finished speaking, and found he was slightly shocked himself at the crude strength of his suggestion; but Dixon's inscrutability was a challenge he was finding it harder and harder to resist.

All he was getting for his blasphemy, of

course, was a shrug and the answer he was expecting: 'I don't have to answer those questions either, Chief Superintendent.'

'No; but thank you for your frankness about yourself, Mr Dixon. That will be all for the present.' Kendrick got to his feet as DS Wetherhead switched off the tape, and glanced at his watch. 'It's been confirmed that Mr Henderson died from cyanide poisoning, and a small forensic team will be arriving here at any moment to examine the outhouses. The use of cyanide is no longer legal for the destruction of wasps' nests and other garden undesirables, but old stocks don't always get safely disposed of.'

Fourteen

'Yes, sir, you'll find my name, Joshua Hodges, in the register at the local chemist – Lucas, in Appleton – if it goes far enough back. Must be twenty, thirty years since I last signed for cyanide, and I can't remember now why I wanted it. Wasps, perhaps, they've allus been a menace around here. I—'

'Mr Hodges,' DS Wetherhead interrupted sternly, 'the cyanide you signed for twenty,

233

thirty years ago is still on a shelf in an out-house – not only not safely disposed of; not even under lock and key.'

The bravado fell away as if scraped off the man's face with a pallet knife. 'I know. I'll feel guilty to the end of me days that I didn't get rid of it, left it loose on the shelf; but I wasn't the one to use it to kill the master.'

'If we'd wanted to murder anyone, it would've been the sister!' The sudden loud interjection of the lad, hitherto slumped beside his boss with a defiant look on his spot-infested face, made both Kendrick and Wetherhead jump. 'Mr and Mrs Henderson was kind, but Miss Henderson's always on at us: nothing's ever good enough; she's always criticizing and interfering. I've sometimes wondered why no one's had a go at *her!*'

'That'll do, Tom!' The older man, lean and weather-beaten and looking the archetypal gardener, his deep-set eyes already haunted, Kendrick thought sadly, by his responsibility for a death, turned on the youth beside him and cuffed his ear. 'You mind your manners and keep quiet unless you're asked to say something!'

'All right, Mr Hodges, all right! No need—'

'So you'd forgotten the cyanide was still in the outhouse, had you, Mr Hodges?' Kendrick enquired.

'What? Jesus Christ, of course I had! It's only because of what's happened and what you've just said that I remember now it was in a corner I've not disturbed for years, along with other stuff I never use or look at ... Oh God, I'll never forgive meself!'

'It was a dreadful oversight, Mr Hodges,' Kendrick insisted reluctantly. 'Even if no one had taken the jar with criminal intent, it looks innocent enough, and anyone who didn't read the very faded label – any child who *couldn't* read it and was playing in and around the outhouses – could have found it, opened it, shaken a little into a hand, liked the smell, tasted...'

'Please, Inspector ... I know. God knows I know!'

'I'm very sorry,' Kendrick said, more willingly. 'You're paying a dreadful price for forgetfulness.'

'What I deserve. But there's nothing more!'

'There's no suggestion of anything more, Mr Hodges.' *At the moment.* Professionally he had to hold on to the proviso, but Kendrick saw the gardener as instrument rather than agent, and didn't expect to be listening to him again until the trial of the man or woman he felt more fiercely by the minute that he must manage to name. 'And I can tell you that your fingerprints weren't on the jar. No fingerprints were. It had been wiped clean. Now, if your jar of cyanide was not the murder weapon, your fingerprints would surely have been on it. Fingerprints don't go away of their own accord. Unless you always wore gloves when you handled it?'

'Oh, my God ... No, sir, I didn't always wear gloves. I knew I should of done, but somehow...'

'It's consistent with your carelessness about safely disposing of the poison, Mr Hodges. However, we won't go over that again.' There could have been other suspects sitting where Mr Hodges was sitting to whom Kendrick might have credited a cunning that would have had them wiping away their own expected fingerprints in order to make him believe some unauthorized prints had been erased, but by no stretch of his imagination could he see the Fifield Place gardener capable of such ingenuity. 'That will be all.'

With the arrival of the forensic team Kendrick had suspended further interviews and asked Mr Dixon as politely as possible temporarily to surrender his mobile phone and remain with DS Wetherhead in the sanctum. He had personally curtailed WPC Johnson's walk about the grounds and sent her upstairs to wait outside Mrs Henderson's bedroom door. He had then taken the WPC's place in the garden, where he had strolled about, trying to feel calm, his path taking him regularly past the outhouses and the forensic investigation so that he could receive regular information on its progress.

When the team's leader had emerged with the jar of cyanide in a bag and given him a verbal resumé of the report she would write, Kendrick had sought out the gardener and his lad and led them, muttering nervously, to the sanctum, where he had asked Mr Dixon, again as politely as possible, if he would be good enough to take a stroll out-side.

Following the departure of the gardeners and a short consultation *à deux*, Kendrick and Wetherhead made their way to the kitchen, where they found one large lady, whose name Kendrick couldn't remember, handing Mr Hodges a steaming mug. In the act of sitting down at the big central table, piled with half-prepared vegetables, Mr Hodges changed his mind, touched the cap he had resumed, and carried his mug speed-ily out through a door that appeared to lead towards the open air.

The distress in the large lady's face as she turned to them told Kendrick that Hodges had done their preliminary work for them.

'Poor Joshua!' she exclaimed. 'He's that cut up!'

'Did you know the jar containing cyanide was on a shelf in the farthest outhouse, Mrs

237

Symington?' DS Wetherhead inquired, and Kendrick marvelled, as he was so often forced to, at his sergeant's retentive memory.

'I did not, sir; but then, I didn't know there was a jar of any kind. That's Mr Hodges's territory and I never went there 'cept when I needed to tell him what vegetables I wanted brought in and couldn't find him about the garden.'

'Would any members of the household go into the outhouses?'

'Well, yes, sir, I suppose, if they was looking for Mr Hodges too. That would be the only reason – 'cept for Miss Henderson, of course: she runs the place and there's nowhere you mightn't find her.' Distress gave way to shock. 'But I wasn't saying ... Heavens above, Mr Policeman, Miss Henderson would never have took that jar, 'cept if she thought it was something else or that it ought to be disposed of.'

'Thank you, Mrs Symington. You've been very helpful. I hope you may be able to help Mr Hodges come to terms with his part in what has happened.'

To both policemen's surprise, Mrs Symington coloured. 'I'll do my best, sir. Mr Hodges and me ... we're both widowed and we've lately got together. I'll try to cheer him up.'

'I feel a bit happier about our gardener

now,' Kendrick said to his sergeant as they went back into the main hall. 'That's a good, strong woman. Now, Fred, the sun still appears to be shining, so we aren't imposing any hardship on the business manager; but better go and ensure, from a distance if possible, that he's all right – after you've hopped upstairs to see how WPC Johnson's doing. I'll go and look for the sister; I'm surprised she hasn't shown herself before now. It's the women who have the motives, Fred – whacking great ones. The wife's been betrayed, and the sister's been threatened with what she sees as the desecration of all she holds dearest. If Dixon's told it as it really is, I can't see why *he* could have wanted to destroy Henderson; and if he was simply fed up, he could have walked away.'

Kendrick found Hermione Henderson in the chapel, kneeling before the altar, her upper arms stretched out along the Communion rail. Wary of her response to his presence even if not disturbed in such an uncharacteristically humble posture, he beat a hasty tiptoed retreat to the doorway and advanced a second time with a heavy tread and a cough, relieved to see that, as he entered the short nave, Hermione Henderson was on her feet and glaring towards the entrance.

'Detective Chief Superintendent Kendrick! Have you come to pray for a flash of insight?'

'I've come looking for you, Miss Henderson. There are one or two further things ... Will you come with me to the library?'

'I'll join you there in just a few moments. All right?' Eyes growing by the second more accustomed to the comparative gloom, Kendrick saw that her ample breast was heaving, and that there was a breathiness in her voice he had been unaware of the day before; but she had, of course, had several hours in which to contemplate the implications of the outrage she had greeted the day before off the top of her head...

'Of course. Thank you.'

She was with them in the sanctum inside five minutes.

'Yes?' she demanded aggressively as she sat down.

'First of all, Miss Henderson,' Kendrick said, without preliminary. 'We now know officially that your brother died from cyanide poisoning. We also know' – he held up a restraining hand as she drew breath for an inevitably hectic response – 'that there was a jar of cyanide on a shelf in the farthest of your outhouses, from which all fingerprints had been removed. It was there from a very long way back and therefore legitimately, but should, of course, have been safely disposed of when its use became illegal, and before that kept under lock and key – oversights that Mr Hodges of course now deeply regrets. Did you know it was there? I gather you take a day-to-day interest in the running of the garden as well as of the house.'

For the moment he had winded her. She sat in silence, glaring from one policeman to the other, the arms that had been stretched in prayer now folded across her bosom as if to hide its agitation.

'Well, Miss Henderson?' DS Wetherhead prompted.

'I heard you.' To Kendrick's surprised relief, the voice was calm. 'I'm just ... It's terrible! I can't take it in. Of course I had no idea it was there. If I'd known, I'd have had Joshua Hodges all round the houses! Leaving a deadly poison on an open shelf! That's criminal in itself!' Having found a pretext for righteous indignation, a state of mind on which she obviously thrived, Miss Henderson was visibly regaining certainty and strength.

'Not officially, but it has been the direct cause of a terrible crime. The only comfort Mr Hodges can give himself is the thought – I suppose, in his circumstances, it would be the hope – that whoever made use of the cyanide would have found it, or some other poison or weapon, elsewhere. Unless ... Do you think Mr Hodges could have used it himself!'

'Of course not! Really, Superintendent! Joshua Hodges has been unforgivably negligent, but in a million years he could never have killed my brother – or anything beyond a rat or a wasp. I'd vouch for that.'

'Thank you.'

'Anyway ... you say there were no finger-prints!'

'The jar had been wiped clean. Miss Henderson, it has been suggested that your brother might have taken his own life – in which case, he would have had to wipe the jar to make it seem that a murderer had been protecting him or herself. Can you envisage that?'

Both policemen awaited the response with some apprehension, expecting an explosion; but to their further surprise Miss Henderson merely looked thoughtful. 'I can envisage him wiping the jar clean simply because he wasn't thinking what he was doing: he's – he was – so stupidly absent-minded. If he killed himself ... Both alternatives are terrible, Chief Superintendent, but I prefer to think that my brother was murdered. Suicide is a sin in the eyes of God.'

So fanaticism ran in the family, Kendrick reflected.

'There have to have been a lot of fanatics among that Bridge bunch.'

Kendrick and Wetherhead stole a glance at one another, only their eyes betraying their amusement.

'I didn't know them, of course, but I should think any one of them could have slipped the stuff into the glass or the carafe while they were all milling around. As I told you, I saw my brother in his sanctum' – Miss Henderson accorded the word a sarcastic emphasis – 'just before he went out to speak to them. I don't remember seeing the water, so it was probably already out there, vulnerable to any weirdo. I'm sorry I can't be of any more help.'

'You've been helpful already, Miss Henderson.' The temptation to add the word 'surprisingly' was strong. 'And you will recognize our dilemma. On the one hand, a roomful of virtual strangers, all apparently adoring the man they called the Enabler—'

'Blasphemy!'

'But the extremes of love and hate can be very close. John Lennon ... And on the other hand ... two women who call the victim Charles: his wife, whom we have been led to believe he betrayed; and his sister, whom he was trying to rob of all she holds most dear—'

'You're quite right, Chief Superintendent; you have to think of Phoebe and me.' This time his surprise was so much greater Kendrick felt it in his face. Hermione

Henderson, recognizing it, gave a short laugh before she resumed: 'I'm not a fool; I know how it has to look – and I've always suspected Charles of being less than a faithful husband. Yesterday ... well, I was so angry with those stupid people who had let my brother get into the ridiculous situation that one way or another killed him; and so sad, Mr Kendrick, though you may not believe it. Blowing my top tends to help me. I'm older than Charles, and when we were young he used to ... to turn to me.' *To love me*, Kendrick thought she had begun to say, and felt his first pang of pity for the large, red-faced woman whose presence dwarfed the room. Brother and sister alike again – in both being larger than life. 'We grew apart, we violently disagreed, but that ... that need – it's never left me, and I'm certain it never left him. Another reason I can't believe he killed himself, Chief Superintendent, is that if he had done, he would have contrived to give me some sort of farewell.'

After she had left, Kendrick and Wetherhead sat in silence.

'I never thought I'd feel like *this* after interviewing that particular witness,' Fred Wetherhead said at last.

'Nor me. Perhaps the fluffy little lady will surprise us in the other direction,' Kendrick responded hopefully.

'Perhaps. Hadn't we better have her in, sir?

We've given her—'

Kendrick's mobile warbled. 'Hold on, Fred.'

Kendrick pulled a sheet of paper towards him, and wrote as he grunted. 'Contents of the will, Sergeant,' he said when he had rung off. 'As we know, the house and grounds became his sister's at the moment of Henderson's death. The wife's been left all the contents of the house – except for the chapel fittings – which I should say would amount to several hundred thousand pounds. Also her brother's money, which I can't think will be anything like as much. Nothing to Dixon, but of course the will was made before The Bridge was founded.'

'So it appears to fit with what you were saying about the women's motives, sir.'

'Yes, Fred. Now, I'll go upstairs myself, relieve WPC Johnson, and escort Mrs Henderson to the sanctum.'

'No sight or sound,' the PC greeted him, relief in her face, as she rose smartly from the bedroom chair DS Wetherhead had found for her. 'I was beginning to feel uneasy.'

'I'll take over. Go back into the garden and look casually for Mr Dixon. If you bump into him and you start chatting, it can't be bad.'

Kendrick could feel the beating of his own heart as he knocked at the fine panelled door, and it was a relief to hear an immediate 'Come in!'

'Chief Superintendent Kendrick!' Mrs Henderson was advancing towards him where he stood in the open doorway, all pink-and-cream femininity, and behind her he had a vague impression of delicate nightwear draped across a shiny satin bed and an adjacent chair. 'Thank you for giving me time this morning. I've taken advantage of it, and been resting. I'm ready now to speak with you. I hope you have received willing co-operation from ... the household.' *From my sister-in-law.*

'We have indeed, Mrs Henderson. Now, if you will be good enough to come down to the sanctum. Please lead the way.'

She seemed to float down the elegant curving staircase, her fingertips touching the polished banister lightly and intermittently. When they reached the sanctum door, she made a forward gesture with an arm from which a light, transparent fabric fell gracefully away. 'Please go first.'

'Mrs Henderson!' DS Wetherhead shot to his feet and, following a nod from his chief, switched on the tape. Mrs Henderson sat down without hesitation and looked from one policeman to the other as they took their seats. Kendrick searched her face as discreetly as he could manage for signs of distress, but found nothing to suggest it beyond, perhaps, the disproportionate size of the blue eyes in the small pink-and-white oval that narrowed so noticeably towards the determined chin – the one feature, he thought, that might indicate that the fluffiness had a firmer foundation than superficially appeared.

'Mrs Henderson, I am very sorry that the circumstances of your husband's death mean that I am unable to leave you to grieve in peace.'

'Thank you, Chief Superintendent. It was clear to me from the moment Charles died that you would have to investigate his death.'

'Do you believe he was murdered, Mrs Henderson? Or that he killed himself?' Thanks to Phyllida Moon, he knew which answer he ought to expect, and that if he received the other, Mrs Henderson would edge ahead of her sister-in-law in his so far personal suspect order.

'Charles would never have killed himself, Mr Kendrick; he loved life too much.' Almost word for word. So far, so innocent.

'But murder!'

'I know. The mere thought is frightful. But I was already fearful for my husband, knowing he could have had so many unknown enemies: the families of the young people who sat at his feet; of the young man who jumped over the cliff—'

'Of the young people – or the young people themselves – whom he seduced.'

Both policemen heard the sharp intake of breath and saw the infinitesimal shudder, but Mrs Henderson's face hadn't changed. 'My husband didn't seduce people, Mr Kendrick, of whatever age. If he held out his arms, they were entered. He was not as other men; he had particular powers.' A very short pause. 'And particular needs.'

A paraphrase of Dixon's apologia. Had they got together before Kendrick and Wetherhead had arrived?

'And you don't feel that the fulfilment of those ... needs might have made your husband vulnerable to murder?'

'Not by those who were privileged to fulfil them, Mr Kendrick; but yes, as I said, perhaps the families ... unable to understand...'

'Thank you, Mrs Henderson.'

Kendrick was aware of the relaxation of the stocky body beside him, and shared his sergeant's relief from the fear that had sat heavy on them both all morning: of having to break the news of a husband's infidelity to his widow within twenty-four hours of his death.

'We can now confirm,' Fred said, after a glance from his chief, 'that your husband died from cyanide poisoning; and that our forensic team have discovered a jar containing that poison on an open shelf in your

248

farthest outhouse. Your gardener has told us that he obtained it legally a great many years ago, and acknowledges that he ought to have disposed of it safely or at least had it under lock and key.'

'When found by my team,' Kendrick added, 'it had no fingerprints of any kind on it and had obviously been wiped clean. Did you know it was there?'

'No.' It could be clever make-up that was maintaining the delicate colouring of her face, but Kendrick suddenly noticed a tick at work under one of her eyes. 'But I never go into the outhouses; I have no need.'

'Unless you're looking for Mr Hodges? I believe you are responsible for the beautiful flower arrangements about the house?'

The look of gratification – the only change in Phoebe Henderson's face since she had confronted him at her bedroom door – told Kendrick it had been a good guess. 'Thank you. Yes. And yes, now I think about it, I suppose if I want to see Hodges about the flowers I may go and look for him, and if I don't find him in the garden, I'll look in the outhouses; but as soon as he sees me at the door he comes out to speak to me.'

'Of course. Mrs Henderson, you don't have to answer this question, but do you envisage yourself and your sister-in-law both continuing to live at Fifield Place?' Kendrick wished he had asked Miss Henderson that question, but there would be another opportunity.

'Oh, yes, Mr Kendrick. We shall manage very well – as we manage now. Hermione will continue to appoint and direct the staff and look after the chapel, and I'll do the flowers and liaise with Mrs Symington and see to the indoor upkeep.'

Listening to the calm voice and looking into the tranquil eyes, Kendrick thought of the other female Henderson and her unexpected control. No overt evidence of grief in either woman, beyond Hermione's touching revelation of her brother's one-time dependence on her. Just ... acceptance. For a wild moment, Kendrick had a mental picture of the two women searching the outhouses together, and was dismayed by DS Wetherhead's first words when Mrs Henderson had left them.

'The women, sir ... Could it have been a conspiracy?'

Pushed, he couldn't believe it. 'No, Fred; but they're running neck and neck.'

They found Mr Dixon and WPC Johnson sitting together on one of the upper terrace seats overlooking the long view.

'We're away now,' Kendrick told them. 'Feel free to come and go as you please, Mr Dixon.' That was not what he had said to the women. 'We shall be speaking to Mrs and Miss Henderson again, and they have told me they will be remaining in the house for the time being.'

'I see.' Another thing Kendrick was unable to interpret was the look of infinite sadness in the hitherto expressionless face.

Fifteen

The attractive young couple sat side by side on the park bench, studying papers the woman had taken out of a briefcase. It was the first really warm day of spring, calm and sunny, and their ungloved fingers touched as they rustled through the pages – touched and sprang apart as if stung, then touched again and briefly interlaced before once more springing apart, on a mutual look of alarm and longing.

The elderly woman sitting the other side of the narrow path observed them through the tinted spectacles that appeared to be directed at the newspaper she was holding, noting the inner hand of each disappear, squeezed down and out of sight between their adjacent thighs, where interlacing could take place unseen.

The contact was short-lived. The woman got to her feet, stuffing the papers back into the briefcase as she rose, and her lips said, 'I can't stand this.'

The man got up too, and said, 'Thursday, then,' loudly enough for the words to carry across the path.

'Thursday.'

'As usual.'

A moment of staring immobility, and then the two young figures were striding off in opposite directions. They were out of sight by the time Phyllida folded her paper, rose from her bench and set off towards the park exit, rejoicing in the temporary relaxation of a straightforward case of marital infidelity. Emotionally exhausted by her involvement with The Bridge, yet dreading the first day empty of a part in the investigation of its founder's death, she had asked Peter for the simple assignment.

'I've got enough for Steve to follow up,' she told him, when she had made the few modifications to her appearance necessary to restore Miss Bowden and had crossed Dawlish Square to the Agency; 'and probably enough to justify John Spellman's worst fears. But before contacting him I think we should let Steve and his camera follow whichever of them he finds the safer and easier when they leave work on Thursday.'

'Agreed.'

'Peter ... I'm worried about Denis Young.

252

He's so disturbed I'm afraid he may do something drastic. I don't suppose there's any more we can do to help our client as a policeman, but he hasn't set a term to Miss Lubbock's occupancy of the Heights flat, and I'd be happy if she could be around for Denis for a while longer. He came knocking the other night; he could come again. And you never know, he might just offer something useful to the police, perhaps without knowing it. Shall I speak to Maurice?'

'He spoke to me an hour or so ago. He'd be grateful if Miss Lubbock could be around the Heights for a while longer, in case any of the young Bridgeites make contact. He spoke a bit wistfully about Mrs Santorini, but I said I didn't see how we could maintain both women, and Denis Young and Miss Lubbock do both live at the Heights.'

'And Miss Lubbock, or Sally – if she can spare any more evenings – can always put whoever it is in touch with Mrs Santorini, if she's the one they want.'

'So long as you're happy for her to be nominally still at the Golden Lion.'

'Of course. You know how I love my Americans. Did Maurice say anything else?'

'He just said it was all one hell of a mess and he was hating it; but I got the feeling – without any evidence – that he knows where he's going. He didn't attempt to hide his delight that The Bridge is more than likely busted, and I think he was wistful again when he said he was glad for the women that a scandal was unlikely. He said we're to keep his private file open, and your hours totted up, so long as Miss Lubbock's at the Heights, and that he'll tell us what he can when he can about the progress of the police investigation.' Peter scratched his head and rolled his eyes. 'It's all incredible, isn't it? Surrealist.'

'And the Agency's made professionally for life.'

'By the Chief of Police – that's the surrealistic bit. And you're made for life twice, Phyllida, d'you realize?' *But you've lost what would make just one life worthwhile.* The thought occurred to Peter after he had spoken, and he cursed his insensitivity as he hastened on. 'I mean, it can only be a matter of time before you're summoned back to the television screen.'

'That's not a certainty, and I don't even think I want it. I got away with my anonymity intact once, but to put it at risk a second time could be a venture too far.'

'You are the most perverse woman I have ever met. Who else would put detective work in a seaside town ahead of fame via television? Anyway, if the summons comes, you'll have to answer it.'

'Don't look so glum. I don't *have* to do

254

anything. It may never happen; and if it does, and I say yes, it'll just be an interlude.'

'Dear Phyllida.'

Miss Bowden's mobile rang at half past one, when she was having a sandwich and coffee in the corner of Mick's small bar. It was Sally, anguished.

'I said I'd be with you – with Miss Lubbock – tonight, and you know I want to be, but some function's come up with Jeremy and he's asked me—'

'Sally, you know I expect Jeremy to come first. Anyway, we'd probably just have sat in the flat, all dressed up and nowhere to go.'

'Which you'll have to do now all on your own.'

'I've done worse, and there are books and television. Don't worry, please; just have a good time.'

'Will you be at the Heights tomorrow?'

'It looks like it. Our client wants me to be around a bit longer, in case a member of The Bridge gets in touch.'

'But Sam Mason won't. So why...'

She shouldn't have been wetly lamenting the end of her involvement with The Bridge; she should have been devising some way of explaining the situation to Sally without explaining it.

'Sally ... There's a bit more in our client's remit than Sam. I'm sorry I can't tell you

255

about it.'

'And I'm sorry I sounded nosey.' How Sally sounded now was excited, rather than nonplussed, by a renewed mystery. 'Especially as it has to be to do with the murder.'

It was impossible to tell over the telephone if Sally's ensuing silence was a silence of expectation. Whatever, Phyllida responded with no more than: 'I'm glad you understand, Sally,' and the sop of an enquiry as to whether Sally would be free the following evening. 'It could be our last.'

'Of course! And I've told Jeremy that, as I can't have tonight, I must have tomorrow. Anyway, he'll be in London.'

'Good. I'll expect you at the Golden Lion. Six?'

'Straight from work. Will you ring Denis tonight if he doesn't contact you?' – somebody else sounding wistful.

'I think it's a temptation Miss Lubbock will be unable to resist. Not that I relish the idea of a tête-à-tête. I'll confine contact to the telephone if I can.'

'Shit. *Sorry!* But I hadn't realized what I could be condemning you to.'

'It's not as bad as that, silly. Please enjoy yourself tonight and don't worry, Sally. That's an order.'

'I'll do my best. See you tomorrow.'

In the event Phyllida decided Miss Lubbock would be déshabillé if and when Denis came to her door, and would therefore explain to him from behind the chain that she was unable to let him in on the grounds of propriety as well as continuing slight ill health. If he didn't ring, she would ring him in the late evening.

So, although she was a prisoner in the high flat, she was a prisoner in her own persona, learning more surely by the minute that she would never again consider her small room at the Golden Lion to be hostile or austere. At least she had overcome her initial sense of being cut off from Jack when she was inside Pickford Heights, and there was the big window to sit by as she intermittently read and watched the descent of the night, and then some television; and, after her supper, dozed. Phyllida was unaware she had gone to sleep until the shrill of the telephone had her leaping to her feet.

It was, of course, Denis, sounding unexpectedly calm. 'I was just wondering how you are now, Miss Lubbock. I feel I've been a bit neglectful.'

'Nonsense, Denis. You have your young life to lead; and I know how very upset you've been: I was so sorry to hear from Sally and her American friend of the terrible thing that has happened. I hope you're beginning to come to terms with it.'

'I doubt I'll ever do that, Miss Lubbock,

but I suppose I'm feeling a bit more able to cope with it.'

'That's very mature. I'm glad to hear it.'

'Are *you* feeling better?'

'Thank you, Denis, I am. I'm even thinking of getting dressed tomorrow, and maybe sniffing the air.'

'That's great. But don't overdo it.'

'I'm not built to overdo anything, Denis, but thank you for your concern.'

'That's all right … Well, goodnight then. I hope to see you before long.'

'Thank you, that would be nice' – if Miss Lubbock's tenancy didn't come to an abrupt end. Phyllida sighed, in a mingling of relief and regret, as she realized that her next-day reassuring report on Denis Young could hasten the decree that it should.

She was eating her breakfast when the national radio news turned local and sent her spoon clattering into her bowl of cereal.

A report has just come in that a body has been found at the foot of the west cliff, close to the place where the body of Stanley Dolby was recently discovered. It is not yet known if the police are treating the death as suspicious.

For a moment Phyllida thought she was going to be sick, watching her mental picture of Denis Young poised on the cliff edge with his mobile at his ear, phoning Miss Lubbock as the last act of his life and quietly exultant in the knowledge that he

258

would never again be an obscure local-government clerk.

'There was a Bridge leaflet in her pocket,' Detective Chief Superintendent Kendrick told DS Wetherhead, glee vying with exasperation in his uncharacteristically animated face.

'*Her* pocket, sir?'

'Yes, Fred. You were expecting it to be Denis Young, weren't you, the only member of the sect who was unable to take control of himself after the murder? But no. Do you remember the girl who wept her way through her interview. "Like Niobe, all tears." '

'Pardon, sir?'

'Just an unnecessary quote, Sergeant.' Kendrick looked down at the papers on the desk in front of him. 'Marian Kershaw. Secretary. Lives alone with a cat. Hope someone sees to it. We can't avoid a scandal now, Fred.'

'No, sir. When was the body discovered?'

'Early this morning, by a dog-walker. The doctor's ventured last evening round about six o'clock, but that's pre-post-mortem, of course. So far as he can see superficially, there are no injuries inconsistent with the force of the fall.'

'You'll not be asking that the possession of the leaflet be kept from the media this time, sir.'

'I will not, Fred. Not to my displeasure, I admit.' *Now that my niece is safe.* Kendrick knew, as they looked at each other for a silent moment, that he and his sergeant were sharing the thought. 'I've just talked to Miss Moon at the Heights and she's agreed to spend the day there as well as tonight. Young could well stay off work with the further shock, and he's pretty well bound to seek comfort. She was as staggered as you were, by the way, that it wasn't Young who took the plunge. I suppose I shall have to hold a press conference once the news of the death – and the Bridge literature – is public knowledge; but for the moment it doesn't call for any further police action. So let's make the best of the hiatus and think and talk about the murder.'

'You've had further thoughts, sir?'

'I don't know, Fred. The women's motives are so equally compelling I can't put one in front of the other. But something...' *Oh, yes, Mr Kendrick. We shall manage very well.* 'I'm inclined to favour the wife on personality, and if it is her, it's all been very sanely and logically worked out. If it's the bluff, in-your-face sister, then I think it would have to be the result of a fanatical devotion to the Church, and over three decades of police work I've learned that fanaticism can distort a nature which, outside the obsession, would shrink in horror from any act of violence. What I'm saying is that I've really no idea, Fred. So how about giving me the benefit of your own gut instincts? It wouldn't be the first time—'There was a tap at the door. 'Come!'

The newest, youngest uniform, a package in his hand. 'Special delivery for the Chief Superintendent, sir – by name. Sergeant Whitson's asked me to say that, despite the "Personal and Private" he ordered it to be investigated because it was bulky enough to hold a device. It didn't. It's a DVD. No one's read the letter that came with it.'

'Thank you, Constable.'

'Thank you, Brown,' DS Wetherhead murmured.

'DVD!' Kendrick said disgustedly, turning the package in his hands. 'We don't have a machine to play it, do we, Constable?'

'I don't believe we do, sir.'

'Then you'd better get one from somewhere, and have it set up in here.'

'I could be a bit more than passive,' Phyllida suggested to Peter on her mobile, when they had ascertained that the Chief Superintendent had spoken personally to both of them, and exchanged expressions of their astonishment that it was not Denis Young who had plunged over the cliff. 'I could ring Denis and leave a message on his answerphone – I know he has one – to call Miss Lubbock when he gets in. When he does, and if it's obvious he hasn't heard the news, she'll invite him in and tell him face to face. If he does know, she'll ask him if he'd like to come round for tea and sympathy.'

'Would you? Could you cope?'

'Not very happily, but I see it as part of the job, and I think Maurice will, too. The best scenario would be if Denis manages to marshal the young ones again at his place, and asks Miss Lubbock to join them. But I'm not hopeful about that.'

'Me neither. Well ... thanks.'

'I'll ring him now.'

There was no reply to her call, which might mean either that Denis had gone to work as usual or was prostrate somewhere with grief, and she said merely that she would like him to ring her back as soon as he got home. Then, still wearing her house-coat and mildly enjoying the unique sensa-tion of being sloppy for a reason, she opened her laptop beside the big window and caught up with some private correspon-dence before allowing herself to bemoan the lack of a daily paper. She had made sure she had an engrossing novel, however, and it was after a poached egg and another coffee that she tried Denis's number again. Her call was again unanswered, but only a few minutes after she had made it she heard heavy, hastening steps in the corridor, which stopped at her door in the moment when there was a repeated knock.

Cursing under her breath as she spilled coffee on the chair arm, Phyllida sprang to her feet, slowing to a measured tread as she approached the door and shouted through it.

'Who is it?'

'It's Denis, Miss Lubbock. I've just heard the most extraordinary news. They let me come home when they saw what it had done to me. Please let me in.'

'Of course.' He hadn't even been home; he'd come straight to the old woman who had befriended him. 'I've been trying to get hold of you since I heard the terrible news too. You'll hear me on your answerphone. Denis ... just give me half an hour, will you; I'm not dressed and I was dozing when you rang the bell.'

'God, I'm sorry, I should have thought ... but the way I was feeling, I just—'

'Of course. No apology needed. But the sooner I bestir myself the sooner I'll be ready to receive you.'

'You're sure that'll be all right?'

'Quite sure. So go home and take some deep breaths and make yourself drink a cup of tea. I'll give you a ring as soon as I'm ready.'

He looked terrible, and the moment he

was in Miss Lubbock's dark, narrow hall he burst into tears.

'Come through, come through.' The assumption of a disguise had never felt so much of a chore, but at least the effort had already proved worth it. 'And sit down. Have you had some tea?'

'Yes.'

'Alcohol?'

'No.'

'Then I'm going to get you a brandy.' That had been another thoughtfulness on the part of Maurice Kendrick and his team: one of the kitchen cupboards had yielded a half-bottle of brandy, three bottles of goodish wine, and some soda water.

'Drink this.'

When he had spluttered over a mouthful, Miss Lubbock said, 'Poor Marian.'

'No!' Denis set his glass down on the table beside him, so heavily that the liquid slopped over and Phyllida found herself thinking that another white ring would hardly be noticed. 'Not poor Marian, Miss Lubbock. Marian's gone with her friend into eternal life.'

'But you told me, Denis – or one of you did, or I read it in your literature – your leader frowned on suicide.'

'Yes, of course. In the general way. But that's where he is now, Miss Lubbock, on that Other Side. And don't let anyone persuade you that he took himself there!' In his excitement Denis sprang to his feet, his eyes shining. 'Our Enabler would never have done that, never have preached what he wouldn't practise himself. Some evil creature killed him, some one who couldn't accept his divine message.' He flopped back into his chair. 'But now ... Marian simply didn't want to live without him, without the inspiration of her life. So she took her friend's hand and followed him. She'll see him again, Miss Lubbock, she'll be with him now! I only wish I had her courage!'

'I'm glad you haven't, Denis. I'm still sure your leader wouldn't want you to anticipate your death, and you know that he'll still be there to welcome you, however many years ahead.' How many other Bridgeites, Phyllida wondered, feeling slightly ashamed as the ridiculous platitudes rolled so effortlessly out, were still such tenacious adherents of their vanished Enabler? And how would Denis Young cope with a future that not only reduced him to the sole role of clerk, but offered him no further props for his faith? His best – his only – bet would be to keep in touch with Charlie so that they could fan the dwindling flame with double breaths...

'Oh, yes, I know that. It's my only hope.'

'I don't really know your young friends in The Bridge, but I'm sure Charlie will be taking it as hard as you are. Why don't you get in touch with her?'

'Charlie...' The reflex wince was quickly followed by a slight gleam of light. 'Yes, Charlie'll be faithful. Not like the others – they'll feel bad for a few days and then they'll shrug, turn to something else. But Charlie and I. And Marian...'

'Who wasn't as strong as you and Charlie, Denis. You'll go through the Valley of the Shadow for a long time, and perhaps you'll never quite come out of it, but you'll cope.' Did Miss Lubbock believe in the guff she was spouting? Phyllida suspected that her temperament was too ironic, and that she was offering it out of kindness of heart. A good woman...

'Yes.' Denis took a longer swig at the brandy, and swallowed it without incident. 'I think I will contact Charlie. At least she'll–'

The mobile phone on the table by the window gave a warble. 'Excuse me a moment, Denis. I'm not at home with these modern devices, but Sally insisted on buying me one.' Miss Lubbock took the instrument gingerly into her hand and brought it warily up to her ear. 'Hello? Who is speaking?'

'You have company,' Peter said softly. 'The expected company?'

'Yes.'

'I hope it won't be difficult – or injurious

266

to the job – if you get rid of him as soon as you can.'

'I don't think so. Why do you ask?'

'I've had an SOS from Kendrick. He wants us in his office asap; but he knows what you're up to today because he asked for it, so he's expecting us to take a bit of time. You've got Miss Bowden with you?'

'Of course.'

'Sorry, I'd no need to ask. Perhaps I can be the doctor, ringing to say I'm on my way round?'

'All right, doctor, if you must, although I really do feel a lot better.'

'I'm coming now.'

'Very well. I know my visitor will understand.'

Sixteen

'Without prejudice,' Detective Chief Superintendent Kendrick said heavily, as DS Wetherhead directed Dr Piper and Miss Bowden to two of the chairs facing the DVD player. 'All I'll tell you now is that the recording you're about to watch arrived for me personally this morning by special messenger – so that you'll have the same open and unexpectant mind that I had. Questions, if any, when you've seen it. Sergeant, if you will; I've no idea how to activate the thing.'

Kendrick flung himself down on one of the other chairs, which groaned at the impact, and when he had switched on, DS Wetherhead took the last, the remote control in his hand.

There was silence and immobility for the few seconds it took for the image to form, but when Phyllida saw the man behind the desk, she gave an involuntary gasp of surprise: Brian Dixon, neatly grey-suited as always, grey-haired, grey-faced, looking gravely into their eyes; sitting behind a desk and framed by unfamiliar objects.

'Detective Chief Superintendent Kendrick,' the rich voice said. 'When you watch this recording, I shall be dead. The instrument of my death is beside me now.' The hidden right hand rose to indicate a dark bottle and a carafe and glass on the desk beside it. 'Another death by water, and another death that I shall have brought about. Yes, I killed Charles Henderson.'

This time both Phyllida and Peter stirred, but Kendrick held up a restraining hand, and they subsided into stillness.

'I have tried to put myself in your position, follow your thought processes, and you will see no reason why I should have murdered my employer. Mrs and Miss Henderson both had motives, but I appear to have none. That is true, personally, which makes it difficult for me to explain – to myself as well as to the police – how and why I determined to kill Charles...

'All I said in my statement about myself was true, Mr Kendrick.' Out of the corner of her eye, Phyllida was aware that one of Maurice Kendrick's outstretched legs had jerked. 'My retirement, my heart trouble, my rather complex reasons for going to work for Charles in his new capacity – which makes it all the harder to explain why I killed him. But I must try, I must do the best I can to make you understand, in the interests of justice.'

'Ah. Justice' – Kendrick, under his breath.

'I killed Charles Henderson because I was eventually forced to realize that he was mad; and in his latest craze it was a dangerous madness: he was the mad priest, the Rasputin, contaminating the minds of the young the way Rasputin contaminated the last of the Romanovs and made their murders inevitable. Two young people have taken their lives. I had decided to take mine before I heard the news just now of Marian Kershaw's death, but this second suicide will make it even easier for me to carry out my decision and has, I think, relieved me of the shreds of conscience that hung about my perception of what I have done.

'Because I am not a man without conscience, Mr Kendrick.' For the first time the upright body leaned across the desk, and both arms came up to support it as a trace of passion appeared in the calm face. 'I am not cruel or dedicated to my own well-being: it was my concern for the well-being of the youthful many that persuaded me to take Charles's life. I realized, overwhelmingly, that what he was doing could not go on.

'So much for the why. Now I have the easier task of confessing the how.' Dixon leaned back, and Phyllida was aware, with short-lived amusement, of the corresponding reflex reaction of his audience. 'I am confident that, through my many and varied business connections, I would have been able to obtain a poison that I could have used without betraying my guilt. Because I had no intention originally, Mr Kendrick, of making this confession, as I shall in a moment be telling you.'

More creakings of chairs, noticeable breathing, again from all four spectators. Peter murmured, 'So why...?' and Kendrick snapped that he would find out.

'Before contacting a possible supplier, I decided to look round the old stables and outhouses at Fifield Place. It has seemed to me that nothing has changed there in the lifetimes of Charles and Hermione, and I thought there was a chance that something toxic might have survived from a more careless age when it was legal to use sledgehammers to crack nuts, deadly poisons to dispose of moles, wasps' nests ... I had a tool that I hoped would open a locked cupboard, but I didn't have to use it: the cyanide bottle was sitting, labelled, on an open shelf, in a far corner of the old stable building farthest from the house. I made my investigations after dark, when Joshua Hodges had gone home, and I remember feeling shocked at the ease with which I had discovered the means of murder and was carrying it up to my room.

'Cyanide, as you will know, is easily soluble and colourless in water, undetectable except for its rather agreeable smell of almond oil. I was relying on Charles being so carried away by his own oratory that he would drink without noticing the odour until too late. That is what happened. But what I was also relying on was his taking his one and only drink as the final act of his performance, as he invariably did at Bridge meetings in the De Luxe cinema. A symbol, he said, of the clear, uninterruptible – so long as one had the insurance of the Bridge' (Phyllida thought she saw irony in the steady eyes) – 'stream of life flowing beneath it. And that is where my plan went wrong.'

Brian Dixon coughed, then poured a little water from the carafe into the glass, smiling as he raised it to his lips.

'Charles had a slight sore throat, and he asked me to take the water into the sanctum so that he could have a drink before he went out to the library to address the faithful. That was the first setback. If he hadn't asked for the water, I would have put the cyanide into it somewhere on my way between the kitchen and the library, where I would have placed it on the table on which it stood when he took his final drink. This would have meant that neither his wife nor his sister would have had any more opportunity of doctoring it than anybody else among those milling about the library in the half-hour before Charles appeared to address them. As it turned out ... both of them were alone with Charles in the sanctum when the carafe was still in there –'

'I knew that was a lie,' Kendrick muttered.

'– and so could have added the cyanide. I was so dismayed by their unintended vulnerability that when I was eventually able to carry the water tray out into the library, I almost decided to postpone my plan to poison the carafe till a later time; but I had screwed my courage to the sticking place, and I knew that every day of Charles's powerful madness was another day of psychological, if not physical, danger for the

young people he had perverted, and I realized that I had to go ahead – with difficulty, as
I had to pause in the tiny lobby between
sanctum and library and Charles could have
been watching me. But, as I had expected,
he was entirely absorbed in his final pre-
parations. I had the dose ready in my pocket
in a small container, and when I stepped out
into the library carrying the tray, the carafe
was primed.

'Then came the second and more serious
setback, the setback that put murder ahead
of suicide as the likely cause of Charles's
death. If he had drunk the poison, as I expected, as the final act of his performance, it
would have been assumed that he had taken
his own life. Of course, Mr Kendrick, you
would have had to look into the possibility
of murder, but I don't think it would have
amounted to a serious investigation. Means,
motive, for suicide would have been so
clearly to hand.' For a moment the steady
gaze wavered and fell to the desk, then rose
again and fastened gravely on its watchers.
'There was another reason why I wanted
Charles's death to appear as suicide. Suicide
– anticipation of the certain bliss to come –
was regularly and severely forbidden by the
Enabler, and I reckoned that if he disobeyed
his own prime injunction, it would discredit
him in the eyes of his adherents and add to
his disappearance to shake them out of their

horrific hero-worship – the hero-worship I had helped to bring into being.'

Brian Dixon bowed his head, and in the instant of silence Phyllida said, 'But I think Phoebe Henderson would have cried murder at whatever point her husband had died.'

Kendrick again held up a hand, but this time it was pointing at the screen.

'Phoebe would have rejected the possibility of murder at whatever time in his oration Charles had died, but if he had died at the time I intended, her accusation would have carried far less weight than it did. You, I am sure, Mr Kendrick, have never seriously considered suicide as a possibility, and until you started to watch this film your suspicions must have been fastened on the two women in Charles's life, given the apparently strong motives each had to do away with him.

'So that is the reason why I am making this confession: to remove suspicion from the innocent, to let Phoebe and Hermione live free of the inevitable shadow of suspicion that, unless I spoke, would have hung over them for the rest of their lives.'

Brian Dixon took his second drink of water slowly, but this time none of his watchers moved or spoke.

'My heart problem is serious,' he said as he put the glass down and took the pill bottle into his hand, caressing it. 'Surgery is possible, but I am told the odds in favour of its success are not very good. But aside from that ... I despise myself for my role in Charles Henderson's latest enterprise; I have no children, and my beloved wife is dead. I'm sorry, Detective Chief Superintendent Kendrick, to have caused you so much trouble.'

The thin smile, and the screen went blank. At least, Phyllida thought with relief, he hadn't killed himself in front of them.

'That's it?' Peter asked.

'Every last bit of it.' Kendrick stretched his long legs even further. 'You probably weren't taking much note of Dixon's surroundings, but he was in his own place – flat in the Barbican. There was a key in the package with the video – the DVD – so we didn't have to break in.'

'He gave the impression of being a tidy man,' Phyllida said.

'He was there. Slumped across the table where we've just seen him sitting. He must have made the recording, then taken the pills, some time last night; preliminary estimates put his death as at least fifteen hours previous.'

'So the women are off the hook.'

'That's right.' Kendrick pulled himself upright. 'And you don't have to go back to Pickford Heights, Miss Bowden. Don't worry' – as both Phyllida and Peter shot nervous glances at DS Wetherhead – 'my sergeant is the one member of my staff who is in my confidence. My professional and my private cases are both closed. Thank you, Miss Bowden, for yet more brilliance above and beyond the call of duty. And you, Dr Piper, for being so generous with her time on my behalf. Please render your account.'

'No champagne this time?' DS Wetherhead commented, when Peter and Phyllida had left.

Kendrick flopped back into his chair. 'No, Fred. It doesn't feel like a celebration. Apart from unproductive slog, we haven't had to do the real work, make the breakthrough. It was made for us. No sense of achievement.'

'I think I feel the same way, sir.'

'I expect you do. And I think you must be wondering why I haven't admitted I was wrong.'

'Not really, sir.'

Kendrick shot his sergeant a suspicious glance, then both men grinned.

'Um. Well, I'll tell you. It's because I can't ever be a hundred per cent certain that I am – am wrong. Dixon's story is impeccable. It can't be disproved. But if you think about it, Fred, the evidence to put him in the frame isn't even circumstantial. There *is* no evidence, beyond what he himself offers.'

'But the case will be closed, sir?'

'Oh, yes. It has to be.'

'He was probably telling the truth, Maurice.'

'I know, Fred. I know it's more than likely that he was; but I also know that he could have died to protect one of those women from justice rather than from mere suspicion. If he did, though, we can hardly expect her to come forward and tell us. Ergo: Brian Dixon murdered his employer and confessed to the murder before taking his own life so that his victim's wife and sister would no longer be falsely suspected of the crime. Go and set up the press conference, Fred.'

As his sergeant left the room with a concerned look, Detective Chief Superintendent Kendrick strode across his office and threw himself into his desk chair, swivelling it so violently that it took two turns before it came to rest facing his view of the sea.

'Kendrick seemed a bit ... well, mechanical, I thought,' Peter commented as they drove away from the station. 'No elation. D'you think it's because he feels a bit flat, the way it's all ended – most of the work done for him, no arrest, and so on?'

'Probably. And I don't think he's sure Dixon was telling the truth; he can't get past the massive motives to murder of the wife and sister.'

'He'll have to go along with Dixon's story, though.'

'I suppose so; but he'll never be privately sure, and even the happy outcome for his niece isn't going to offset that uncertainty in a man like Maurice Kendrick.'

'What do *you* think, Phyllida?'

'I think Brian Dixon was telling the truth; but I can't be sure of it, any more than Maurice can. Peter, before we put all this to bed, there's something else, if you agree. Something I'd like to ask Steve to do...'

'Hello, Sam.'

'Denis Young!'

'Sam ... Please...'

He looked dreadful, Samantha thought: even thinner, eyes like holes burned in a white blanket; pathetic.

'You look dreadful.' The ready sympathy she felt for small, unhappy animals was coming on-line. 'I was ... very sorry to hear about what happened.'

'Yes. It was awful. But you weren't there. I noticed. Why did you go?'

Split-second compassionate decision. 'I suddenly felt ill. I ran out for some fresh air, and to get some peppermints out of the car, and ... and I was sick in the car park.' She just couldn't add to the misery drooping in front of her. 'I felt better after that, but not well enough to go back in, so I took myself

278

home and went to bed.' One frail effort. 'It was awful timing, but it was out of my hands. Especially annoying 'cos I was all right by the evening.'

'Well, you were spared sight of the tragedy. We're all devastated. Well, need I say? We're still talking about meeting regularly – well, we young ones – but I don't know; people are so fickle, Sam. Charlie would keep going, and poor Marian would've and I hope you will, but the others...'

So he was still hooked, Sam realized in amazement. For her, The Bridge and all that had accompanied it had vanished into a distant past the moment she had felt the Enabler's breath on her face, and it was hard to think herself back into the mindset that still had hold of this wretched boy.

'Denis, I'm so sorry.'

'Thank you. And if you really are, there's something you can do. We – the young ones – are meeting on the cliff top near where ... where Stan and Marian went over. That's why I'm here, to ask you to join us; I knew you'd be coming out of school about now. I tried to contact Sally at the Heights via Miss Lubbock, but there was no reply.'

'Oh, Denis.' She would have to go. She wouldn't be available for any more meetings; she'd put him off one way or another via the telephone, but she couldn't deny the poor creature his moment of drama, make that white face flinch. 'Yes, I'll come. What time is the meeting?'

Denis looked at his watch. 'Five o'clock. Everyone's asking to leave work early as ... well, as a mark of respect, and everyone was confident they'd not have any difficulty. I went into work specially early – anyway, I didn't want to be alone at home – so I didn't have to ask for time off. So you'll come?'

'Yes, I'll come.'

'Thanks. That means a lot to me. We can walk, or we can drive as far as the road goes. I've got the car' – Denis gestured behind him – 'but there's time to walk.'

'Let's walk.' Denis's company would be easier on foot in public than side by side in the privacy of a car. 'Your car'll be OK where it is.'

'I hoped you'd say that. It's a lovely day.'

'Why don't you give yourself a holiday?' Samantha asked, as they turned down the first road that led towards the sea. 'I'm sure a break would help just now.' It was somehow difficult to make herself look at him, and it was out of the corner of her eye that Sam saw the rise and fall of his shoulders.

'It won't matter where I am,' he said 'It'll be as hard. And here ... well, there's you and the rest of them.'

The invitation to tell him that there wouldn't be her was a tempting one, but

Sam resisted it on the thought that she did not want Denis's mood to deteriorate further on this enforced one-and-only time alone with him.

'Well, you know best what you want, of course, Denis. I'm sorry, one shouldn't try to tell other people how to run their lives.'

'That's all right. At least it shows an interest. The worst thing is ... nothing.'

Which was probably what he would get from now on, Samantha reflected – another reason for her not to show too much sympathy, seeing that she wouldn't be following it up.

'But you wouldn't know about that, Sam.'

'Of course I would. Everyone does, at some time in their lives. But it passes. Sorry again, Denis; this isn't the time for a sermon. Look, let's just walk, and breathe the fresh air. I don't think talk helps at the moment. Unless it's trivial, or about something outside oneself, like what books or films or television programmes one likes.'

'Hard to concentrate at the moment. Hard to care.'

'Of course. But it'll come back. Just look at that sky!'

At least they were walking briskly, and had turned west towards the descending sun, a huge orange ball gentle enough to be looked at direct in brief glances. The tide was almost in, and the tiny wavelets gleamed copper.

'I don't think I'd ever feel entirely right living away from the sea,' Sam said as they marched along. 'At least, not in the long term. I'd always have to know I was eventually coming back to it.'

The shrug again. 'Sea or no sea, it's all the same. The water that matters is the water that flows under the Bridge: the water of life.'

'And the Enabler has crossed the Bridge,' Samantha managed, with a huge effort. 'He's safe.'

'Yes!' The sudden access of energy beside her was palpable. 'And he didn't anticipate his crossing; it was arranged for him, so he's in total bliss.'

'Denis...'

'Yes?'

'Denis, you've just said, the Enabler's in total bliss because he didn't choose to cross the Bridge before his time. You'll remember that, won't you, when you feel ... well, especially depressed. You won't be tempted to ... to follow Stan and Marian?'

'Me!' Denis stood stock-still for a moment in his surprise. 'Not me; I haven't the courage. And anyway, I wouldn't be so stupid as to do the one thing the Enabler said I mustn't. I mean, that would be the most terrible betrayal, whatever happened to me on the other side.'

'Yes. Of course. I'm very pleased to hear you say that. We ... we just have to hope for the best for Stan and Marian.'

'Stan ... Marian'll be all right.'

'What makes you say that?'

'I just ... I just feel it. Nearly there.'

They could see now where the road ahead of them petered out into a sandy track bisecting springy turf starred with hardy sea-edge plants in white and pink. At first there were cottages to their right – from one of which the witness to Stan's death had emerged – but these, too, soon came to an end and there was nothing but sky and sea and grass.

No people.

'We must be early.'

Denis glanced at his watch. 'We are. Shall we go a bit nearer, try to commune with Marian, try to feel how she felt?'

'Not too near, Denis. I get giddy when I'm near a big drop. Let's stop here ... Denis! What are you doing? Let me go!'

'No, Sam. You must let me help you. The way I helped Marian. She let me help her; she hardly struggled at all when I brought her to the edge, and when I helped her over she flew down like a bird. With me helping you, you'll join her in bliss.'

'Denis ... *Help!*'

'No one to hear you, Sam. No one else coming, you see. It's just you and me. Be like Marian: don't struggle too much. I don't want to hurt you.'

Even in her panic, even in the worst moments she had ever spent, she was amazed at his strength; but of course ... the strength of a madman was legendary. There was an unattractive spot beside his nose, oozing pus; but she said, 'Denis, if we leave the cliff edge together we can ... we can be together. Keep the faith. You and me ... Please, Denis.' He had her hands behind her, in a lock that was agony if she tried to move.

'Ah, Sam.' The voice now was reproachful. 'If only I could believe you. But I can't: I know how you feel about me – how they all feel, or felt. Even Marian ... she didn't want to be with me; but I was magnanimous: I gave her a gift that she didn't deserve. You don't deserve it either, Sam, but I shall give it to you: eternal bliss. I'm going to send you into eternity! Just grasp your friend's hand, and I'll see you across the Bridge!'

'No! *No!*'

She was screaming now, struggling despite the pain, but they were moving steadily nearer that abrupt edge where the green grass so suddenly ended. Nearer and nearer...

Then she was flying across the grass, violently propelled: *away from the edge*. A man's voice was saying, 'Oh no you don't!' as Denis was rugby-tackled to the ground,

284

where he lay writhing and stretching out his hands towards the precipice over which he had so nearly cast her.

'We sent you to *protect* Denis Young,' Peter said, scratching his head and smiling bemusedly. 'Phyllida was worried he might do something drastic to himself, and persuaded me to extend the budget to cover your shadowing of him until she felt the danger was over.'

'I'm feeling the way I think Maurice Kendrick was feeling yesterday,' Phyllida said ruefully. 'My benign influence on events was purely arbitrary. The criminals in this case seem to have made all the running.'

'But they ran into the sand in the end,' Steve pointed out. So elated by the biggest input he had yet contributed to an agency case, he had managed for the first time to maintain his careless pose leaning against Peter's desk. 'And talking of sand ... I think chummy changed his mind when I got him round the knees, and began to think that even the forbidden way across his precious Bridge would be better than facing the music on this side of it.'

'I don't know.' Phyllida was pondering as she spoke. 'Think about it: he's ensured that he'll never, ever be an obscure local-government clerk again. By this evening everyone in Britain will have heard of him, and he'll

285

be under the spotlight for the rest of his life.'

'He knew he couldn't get anywhere personally with Samantha Mason,' Peter took up. 'Any more than he could with Marian whatsername. But poor crazy Stan showed him there was one way he could have power over them: the power of life and death. If Steve hadn't been there, I think there would have been other young women falling over the cliff. A serial killer in the making.'

'He couldn't pull 'em, so he pushed 'em,' Steve pronounced.

'I'd say your summing up was spot on, Steve.' Peter reached down into the cupboard that always made Phyllida think of Mary Poppins's carpet bag, and brought out a bottle of champagne and four glasses. 'We may have been more passive than active for once – except for Steve – but it seems to me that the outcome all round is pretty good.' Under his white handkerchief the cork popped gently. 'Steve, go and ask Jenny if she'd care to join us.'